The Secret of Saturn's Rings

A Science-Fiction Novel

The Secret of Saturn's Rings

BY DONALD A. WOLLHEIM

Cecile Matschat, *Editor*
Carl Carmer, *Consulting Editor*

HOLT, RINEHART AND WINSTON
New York · Chicago · San Francisco

99517-0110

Printed in the United States of America

To my daughter Elizabeth

Galileo's Demon

WITH the exception of Mercury and Venus, every planet
in our solar system has at least one or more moons
attending it, but one and only one planet has rings.
That is Saturn, the sixth child of the sun in distance
and the second largest, exceeded in size only by mighty
Jupiter, its nearest neighbor sunward.

Though Saturn is one of the planets easily visible to
the naked eye, and therefore one that has been known
to men from the dawn of history, its mysterious and
amazing rings were first discovered only when Galileo
Galilei turned his newly invented telescope upon Saturn
in the year 1610. His little crude spyglass was responsible
for many astonishing discoveries such as the four largest
moons of Jupiter, the crescent shape of Venus (at certain
times of the year), the mountains of the moon, and many
others, but the rings that encircled Saturn were easily

the strangest sight of all—and became the only one that Galileo finally refused to admit!

When that pioneering astronomer first saw these rings they were presenting their flat, wide and glowing surface toward the Earth and were instantly noticeable. But the next time he looked, it was two years later and the planet had shifted its position in regard to Earth in such a way that only the very thin edge of the rings was facing us. Since this edge is only between fifty and seventy miles thick, whereas the width of the rings is over forty thousand miles, Galileo's small telescope simply couldn't see the thin line that marked their existence. To the Italian scientist, the rings had simply vanished! Perhaps, he thought, they were never anything but a product of the imagination! Perhaps, he went on, the rings were only a trick of the Devil! He cried out, "Is it possible that some demon is making fun of me?" Never again would he dare look at Saturn, and to the day he died he refused to admit a belief in that which his own telescope had shown him in 1610!

But we know the rings exist, and, if conditions are right, they can be seen with even small hand telescopes or strong binoculars. The rings are believed to be composed of millions and millions of tiny fragments, particles of matter similar to the planets, save that instead of combining to form one sphere they remain loose and flowing around Saturn like endless streams of dust. The rings appear solid to the eye, but this is a deception. A few years ago an astronomer was able to observe a star as it moved behind the rings. Had the rings been solid, the star would have vanished in eclipse. But some of its glow continued to be seen even through the rings themselves! This gave proof that the rings are neither solid nor even too tightly packed. It also demonstrated that there could be no moonlets larger than three miles in diameter. Probably the ring-particles range between objects the size of one's fist to midget moonlets of a half-mile or so in diameter.

Under the circumstances, it is likely that such an expedition as that of Bruce Rhodes and his father in this book will take place some time in the next several centuries. The rings of Saturn are not so closely packed as to make a cautious entry into their midst an impossibility. Since they circle their planet at calculated speeds, the various components of each must likewise move in an orderly and relatively stable progression. Certainly the temptation to explore them will be overwhelming to the first space fliers to reach far Saturn. For the solution of their nature and origin may prove to be the most valuable key to the secret of the beginning and the end of Earth itself!

There are three major rings. The innermost one is very dark and is known therefore as the "crepe" ring. About 11,000 miles wide, it begins only 6,000 miles from Saturn's surface. The middle ring is 18,000 miles wide and is the brightest, its most luminous part being its outer edge. A gap of some 2,200 miles, known as Cassini's Divide, separates this from the outermost ring, which is 11,000 miles wide.

Just why these rings vary in speed and brightness, just what differences there are between them, are all secrets which science will have to leave to the Bruce Rhodes of the future to answer.

D. W.

Contents

Chapter 1 Luna Launching Rack

BRUCE RHODES was in for a terrible shock on the very day that should have been one of the happiest of his life. It was high-school graduation day, a day when the boys in his class came in for the last time, held their final assembly, received their diplomas and were given their entrance listings for college. Bruce had always been popular, one of the best boys in his class, gaining high marks in his astronomy and space-engineering classes, and qualifying for entry into the special space-fliers' courses at the state college.

But on that morning, when the exams were all over and it was just a matter of waiting around until assembly was called, Bruce was surprised at the sudden hush that came over his classmates as he entered their room. Instead of greeting him, they were gath-

1

ered in several little groups whispering among themselves. They were giving him rather unfriendly glances as he came in. A few nodded coldly and continued to ignore him otherwise.

Bruce was puzzled. He walked over to one of the boys who had been a close friend. "What's up? Something eating you fellows this morning?"

The other boy looked at him. He had always liked Bruce, who was sixteen like himself and a fellow member of the school basketball team. "Don't you know?" he asked slowly.

Bruce looked at him in wonder. "Know what? Is there something I've done that's bothering you fellows?"

The other chap shook his head slowly. "Not you. Your father. After all, you don't expect us to be keen about this dirty business, do you?"

Bruce was utterly baffled. He grabbed the other boy by the arm. "What are you talking about? What about my dad?"

His friend was amazed. "You mean . . . you haven't seen the papers . . . you don't really know?" At Bruce's headshake, he reached into his desk and pulled out a copy of that morning's newspaper, folded to a column on the front page. Bruce took it. As he read, he felt cold sweat break out, and he felt as if the bottom of his world had fallen out.

"Chief Scientist Fired by Terraluna," said the headline, and went on: "It was announced today by the directors of the Terraluna Corporation, the only authorized organization engaged in exploring and

mining the moon, that the famous Dr. Emanuel Rhodes, chief of their research bureau and responsible for many of their remarkable mining achievements, had been discharged three months ago.

"Terraluna released a statement to the press today charging that Dr. Rhodes had betrayed certain company secrets to parties opposed to the moon-mining development, had attempted to prevent further work by the company, and was engaged in hindering a most important project which Terraluna declared would immensely benefit all humanity. They said that they had been forced to make public Dr. Rhodes' disgrace because of his present efforts to attack the company's good name and intentions."

Three months ago! But Bruce had not had a word of this. His mother had said nothing to him. His father he had supposed to have been on duty at Terraluna's great mining domes on the moon. The fact that his father was world-famous as the inventor of the robot mining prospector, and of dozens of other atomic developments in interplanetary work, had been the pride of Bruce's young life. And now—disgrace. The boys of his day, in the early years of the twenty-first century, had always regarded Terraluna as the biggest thing one could hope to work for. Its mines on Luna, its expeditions on the asteroids, represented the highest pay and the most exciting work. And Bruce's father had been the head of their most exciting section, the department of new projects.

How Bruce got through the rest of that morning he could never remember. Somehow, automatically,

he went along with the rest of his class, feeling the
silent rebukes of his classmates. He got his diploma
from an unsmiling principal, felt the slackening of
applause when his turn came to go up and get it. He
managed to leave school at last and took the air-bus
directly home.

He dashed through the door of his house, looking
for his mother. He found her reading a radio message
that had just clicked off their automatic newscaster
projector. She looked up at him and handed him
the message. It was short and said that Bruce was
to come to the United Nations spaceport in Colorado
without delay. It was signed by his father.

"What's it mean? Where's Dad?" he asked.

His mother smiled. "Don't believe everything you
read. Your father knew what he was doing. You haven't
much time. Pack up and hurry. I won't be able to go
with you, because I have things to do here, but I'll
expect you back in a couple of days."

As she urged Bruce toward his bedroom to start
a quick packing, he asked, "But is Dad back here on
Earth? How come I didn't see him?"

"He'll explain all that to you. These are very, very
serious matters."

Bruce hastily threw some changes of clothes into a
bag, took the fare money his mother gave him, kissed
her good-by. As he started for the air terminal to
catch the next express plane for the spaceport, she
called one more word of warning after him. "Don't
talk to anybody about who you are or where you're
going. Especially not Terraluna people."

All during the next two hours, when his jet plane was hurtling across the land, with its cargo of bored passengers, businessmen commuting, vacationers anxious to get to their goal, Bruce kept silently to himself. For a while he had time to think, to catch his breath.

How suddenly his life had been torn apart! At one moment, Terraluna was the pride of his life, a company he had always expected to work for. Now he felt like an outcast, yet he knew that his father must be able to tell a different story. The newspaper account could only be the company's side of the affair.

Space flight was the great thing in the lives of all the people of Bruce's day. Beginning back in the middle of the previous century when the first rockets had landed on the moon, a combination of brilliant scientists, daring adventurers, and imaginative businessmen had advanced man's frontiers outward through the solar system. The moon had proved a rich source of atomic fuels and rare metals, and the mining centers that had been set up there by Terraluna, the pioneer organization that had financed and operated the first explorations, were the wonders of the ages. Terraluna's ships had spiraled inward to prospect the strange seas and cloudy continents of Venus; one ship had already touched on the boiling deserts of Mercury. Other ships had reached ancient Mars, and many were working the rich deposits to be found in the asteroids. The moons of Jupiter had been pioneered, but beyond that no ship had ever gone.

Bruce's father had been among the early science

pioneers. He had been with Terraluna for over thirty
years and had been for many years their head of research, a man held in high honor in the world. To
Bruce it was unthinkable that his father could have
fallen. Yet he could not doubt the evidence of that day.

It was not the first time that Bruce had been to the
UN spaceport in the Rocky Mountains of Colorado.
He had been there before in past years, after one of
his father's brief vacations back at home. He and his
mother had gone and waved good-by to his dad as the
Terraluna-chartered rocket had taken off with its load
of moon miners and engineers. But this time he
stepped down from the jet express by himself.

No crowd of miners and their families were present
today as in the past. Only Bruce got off, and the jet
roared on its way to its next stop, leaving him alone
at the entrance to the little terminal.

Carrying his bag, he walked into the waiting room.
A familiar gray-haired figure was waiting there, and
they rushed to each other in greeting. Bruce's father
was tall, strangely tanned by the harsh rays of the unprotected sun on the moon's surface. But today Bruce
noticed the tired lines on his brow, and a look of
tension that seemed unwilling to permit the broad
smile with which he usually greeted his son.

Without further delay, Bruce's father took him by
the arm and steered him to a waiting car. "Don't ask
too many questions right now, Bruce. I'll get a chance
to explain things in a little while. There's still some
important work I must complete in the next hour be-

fore I will have a little time to spare. Meanwhile, Waldron here will show you over the ship."

Waldron turned out to be a young man wearing spacehand overalls, who was waiting in the car. He turned to Bruce, gave him a single narrow glance, shook hands rather limply. "Glad to know you," he said.

Bruce returned the greeting and after that the three rode in silence, as Waldron drove the two-wheeled, teardrop-shaped ground car away from the terminal and onto the twelve-mile road to the base of the launching racks.

They made the trip in a few minutes, reaching an enclosure at the base of a towering peak. There they got out, passed through a gate at which was stationed an armed guard in UN police uniform. Dr. Rhodes signed Bruce in, and gave his son a card.

"This will identify you. As you see, this is all top-secret work. Waldron will take you out to look over the ship while I get back to the computing rooms and chart our course."

"When are you going to take off?" Bruce asked quickly as his father started away.

"As soon as possible," the old engineer called back. "In an hour perhaps!"

Waldron pointed to a gleaming vessel already standing on a long arrangement like a railroad flatcar. Bruce knew this was the trolley by means of which the space ships were rolled into place on the launching rack. The two walked over to it.

"Whose ship is that?" asked Bruce, as he noticed that it bore none of the markings of Terraluna or any of the standard space lines.

"It's a special United Nations exploration craft. It's being loaned to your father for this trip. It's almost completely ready," Waldron replied. "Come on inside. There's still some work I've got to complete."

Bruce noticed a tank truck still pumping atomic rocket fuel into the ship's tanks. "How many men are going along?" he asked.

As they climbed the ladder to the entrance lock, Waldron answered, "We're carrying a crew of five, including your father. Two spacehands, myself one of them, an astrogator, a pilot, and Dr. Rhodes as captain."

They entered the ship. It was narrow and cramped, being built for endurance and having most of its space taken up with fuel storage tanks and equipment. Waldron proceeded to the engine room in the rear, a small chamber where the exposed tubes of the various connections were open to survey and where checks could be made directly by crew members on the operation of the various flows and wirings.

"Wait a second," Waldron said. "There's a job I have to do before I can show you the rest of the ship." He glanced at a wrist watch anxiously, then knelt down, picked up a wrench from a wall rack and began to unbolt the cover over the center wall, the one that had meters of direction and speed which duplicated those in the master control chamber at the nose of the ship.

The panel unbolted, Bruce saw that the complicated wiring was exposed, a very neat and exact pattern of many colored wires and tubes. It looked very ship-shape to him.

As it happened, Bruce had studied the wiring on the dummy ship in the school space class, and he was pleased to recognize how exactly the scheme was duplicated.

Waldron evidently was not so pleased. He stood for a moment staring at it, then, taking pliers in hand, carefully wrenched loose several of the wires and began to reconnect them.

Bruce watched him, puzzled. Somehow what he was doing didn't seem to make much sense. If anything, it seemed to him that Waldron was making connections that were simply completely wrong. After all, the wires were of different colors, the points of connection were very clearly marked and had seemed to be correct in the first place. Finally Bruce spoke up:

"I don't understand how you can expect to get the correct reading for that with the wires as you have placed them. I don't claim to be a mechanic, yet that blue wire is plainly marked as coming from Tank Five. You have attached it to the meter listed for Tank Three. How will the pilot know?"

Waldron glanced at him sharply. "Mind your own business!" he snapped. "I know what I'm doing!"

Bruce's nerves had been on edge all that strange day. He wasn't used to being treated like that and he knew he was right. Now a sudden suspicion surged through him.

"I still don't think you're doing the right thing. It doesn't make sense."

Waldron gave another wire a vicious twist, turned and said, "Why don't you just keep quiet? In fact, why don't you get out of here until I finish?" He raised the wrench furiously in a threatening manner.

"I won't," he said slowly, "and I am going to report this business as soon as I find someone else in this crew!"

"Oh yeah!" yelled Waldron, losing all reserve. The spacehand made a sudden thrust at Bruce with the wrench. The boy had expected it however, side-stepped and swung his fist. In a moment all the pent-up emotions of the day came to the surface. With a zest he waded into Waldron, grabbing his arm, punching him in the stomach, and crowding him back with another flurry of fists.

Waldron broke suddenly, dropped the wrench and ran out of the engine room, down the short corridor, and leaped through the open space-lock door. When Bruce got after him, he saw the spacehand heading for the car lot, evidently planning to make a quick escape.

Dr. Rhodes popped out of the charthouse nearby and stared after Waldron. Then he turned and ran up to Bruce in the ship. "What was that about?" he called.

Quickly Bruce explained, and his father went with him to the engine room to see. He was visibly shocked. Taking out a handkerchief, he mopped his forehead.

"That was quick thinking, son," he said. "You were right. It was an attempt at sabotage. With the dials indicating the wrong tanks, we'd have been lost in space within days."

Dr. Rhodes picked up the wrench and pliers and started to reconnect the wires carefully. "We're going to be shorthanded," he said softly. "I don't know where I'm going to get someone to replace Waldron who can be trusted, and in such a short time. I plan to take off in the next hour."

Bruce looked at his father, then said to him, "Suppose I take Waldron's place? I've studied space ships and astronomy in school and by myself. I'm strong. And you know you can trust me."

Dr. Rhodes lowered his pliers and looked long at him. He seemed to struggle with himself. "I have no right to ask you," he said. "It will be a very difficult trip. Who will be left to take care of your mother if we don't return?"

Bruce pressed his offer, his heart beating. "Mother will be proud of us whatever happens. I don't know where you are going, but I'm sure it must be of real importance. Let me come along as the junior space-hand."

Dr. Rhodes nodded slowly. "Yes, I know your mother would never say no. And the trip is important. It may be the most important trip ever made. It may mean life or death for the whole world. I guess you will do."

The boy's heart bounded with joy. And then he

asked the one question he had failed to ask so far. "Where are we going, Dad?"

The old engineer smiled briefly, then his face became quiet and sober. "We're going to Saturn," he said.

Bruce's eyes opened wide. The ringed planet of Saturn! It was beyond the farthest rim of human exploration! But what possible reason could there be for this terrible urgency?

Chapter 2 Slide Into Space

A TRIP to Saturn would represent a longer journey from Earth than had ever been made before. It had been Bruce's belief, from things he had been taught in school about space ships, that a trip of that distance was still considered beyond the ability of the spacecraft that existed up to then. If his father was indeed going to try to make such a record-breaking flight, why the secrecy, and what special plans did he have?

These thoughts brought Bruce's mind back to the first problem—why was his father in trouble, what did Terraluna want, why the hurry? When he regained his tongue from the excitement of being accepted as a crew member on this flight, he bombarded his father with these questions.

Dr. Rhodes nodded. "I'd better explain the situation to you." He glanced at his watch. "We have a little time yet. I believe our course is charted by now, and Garcia can do the checking of the figures. Come forward."

The engineer led the way to the control room at the craft's nose, and there they sat down in the padded chairs that space fliers use. Dr. Rhodes rubbed his forehead a moment, then began:

"I suppose you've seen the papers today, with the story that Terraluna gave them about firing me. This represents their last effort to stop this trip. Up to now they've kept silent and fought this thing behind the scenes.

"To start at the beginning, a couple of years ago I was asked by the directors of the lunar mining project to devise some method of reaching the deep core of the moon. Up to now, our mining has not gone down more than about ten miles. We've taken in a lot of valuable material, tons of diamonds, and so forth, but it was believed that at the very center of the moon there would be rich deposits of the heavier and rarer metals, uranium, radium, platinum, and so on.

"The moon is very light, as you know. It hasn't got the solidity of Earth; most of it is such light rock as pumice and ash and layers of meteor dust. There are huge empty bubbles through the moon's interior, like giant caves dozens of miles across. When the moon was first created, it was liquid hot like all the planets, but as it cooled, the heavier elements sank toward the center. Being so much lighter than Earth, they sank completely down; on our own world, there are heavy metals that remained near the surface. Not so on the moon.

"So it seemed right to believe that there would be some very valuable findings if we could figure out how to mine at the moon's heart one thousand miles below its surface. This was what I was asked to invent.

"I worked at that problem for a long time, until I finally solved it. I invented a system of rapid-fire atomic blasting, a sort of directed self-renewing series of atomic bombs that would blast off in any direction we wanted and continue as long as needed. I worked out the idea behind this and showed what was necessary to make the actual machinery to do this.

"For this work, I was praised and rewarded financially by them. But as for me, I was not quite through. I went on with my studies to determine just what might be the result of such deep-core atomic blasting. I ended my calculations four months ago.

"I found that the moon is too light and too loose a structure to allow that type of blasting safely. A little atomic blasting on the surface for mining purposes is all right. But if a series of such incredibly powerful explosions were set off near its center, the result would be the crack-up of the moon itself."

Bruce was listening, his head resting on his elbow, which was propped up against a panel of the controls. He nodded to show his father he had understood thus far.

"The moon is not like a free planet such as Mars or Mercury. It is a satellite, revolving around a bigger and heavier world, our Earth. Because of this, it is subject to great strains from the gravitational pull of the Earth. You know how the moon's pull draws the water of the ocean to cause our tides. If the moon had oceans, it would have even greater tides due to its lesser gravity and the Earth's stronger pull. But even without water, it is affected by this pull. Only it is the very mass, the rocks and stuff of which the moon consists, that feels this tidal pull from Earth.

"Besides its normal motion in space, every particle of the moon feels a constant draw from Earth, is made looser from its brothers by this draw. The moon is fragile.

"Astronomers have shown that someday, billions of years from now, the moon will fall closer to the Earth and be torn apart into tiny fragments. These fragments will fly around the Earth and finally form a sort of ring around our world. My figures showed that atomic blasting at the moon's core would shatter the whole satellite into such fragments now. *The moon would burst apart like a bomb!*

"Some bits of this lunar bombshell would hit the Earth, causing great damage. Most of these pieces would continue to fly along the moon's orbit and form a ring. But the effect would be just as terrible as if they had struck our world.

"With the release of the moon's pull, the tides would cease and the waters of the world equalize. This will flood great parts of the world's surface, wipe out hundreds of cities and drown millions. Great quakes will probably destroy the rest as the Earth's bulk is released from the strain of its satellite and re-adjusts itself. I would say that probably nine-tenths of humanity would die; certainly civilization would be totally destroyed!"

Bruce gasped. "But surely Terraluna realizes that! They certainly wouldn't want to risk that. They must have agreed with your discovery!"

Dr. Rhodes shook his head. "They did not. They refused to accept my figures, plain as they were. They are going ahead with the building of the deep-core atomic blaster!"

Bruce was horrified. "But how could they? Why should they do such a thing?"

Dr. Rhodes smiled grimly. "People are sometimes blinded by their own selfishness, Bruce. Terraluna wants to get at that treasure at the moon's heart. Its directors are not interested in how they get it, they want only the results. When I presented my studies of what would happen, they could not bring them-selves to believe it. They called it wild, imaginary, just the product of an old man's frightened mind. They had some of their scientists, men of my own staff actually, go over the figures. These men sought only for their own advancement, they wanted to keep on the good side of Terraluna's directors, they felt they could take a chance with Earth's welfare. So these men made light of my findings, said they were extreme, ridiculed the possibility involved, and denied the discovery.

"I argued and I fought, but after a month I realized that I could not persuade Terraluna to give up this project. Finally, I returned to Earth.

"I went to the United Nations and spoke to the members of their Committee on Scientific Research. They held secret sessions with me, and they had my figures checked by various great scientists of the world. These men did not all agree. Finally, the United Nations authorities told me I would have to present more proof of my beliefs before they would issue orders to Terraluna to quit their deep-core project."

"But how could you do that?" asked Bruce. "What more could you do?"

"I'm coming to that now," his father answered. "I showed them that there was one place in our solar system where factual evidence could be obtained. That was on the planet Saturn, which has a ring around it. If that ring could be shown to be the result of the collapse or explosion of a satellite, then my figures would be accepted and Terraluna stopped. Nowhere else could any further facts be obtained to prove my point.

"The UN people went into further argument about that, but the issue is very important and there is so much at stake that they finally agreed to let me try to get that evidence. They agreed to lend me a space ship if I could figure out how to reach Saturn with our present type of space rocket. I knew a way and showed them.

"This ship is the one they lent me. It has been fueled, our course is now worked out, and with you the crew is complete."

Bruce nodded, then asked, "But then why did Terraluna tell the papers you were a traitor? Aren't they willing to let you find proof? After all, surely they can't afford to risk the destruction of two worlds?"

The old engineer frowned, stood up. "You know the answer to that. The directors are blind with their own selfishness. They are furious at my interference. They are more determined than ever to go ahead and they are going to try to stop me from ever getting such proof.

"They released their own false story to the press today, to create public hatred toward me. Thus if this ship fails to return or otherwise fails to make its trip, the public will not be angered. They will not care what happens to a 'traitor' scientist.

"The second step you yourself stopped. They had managed, with their tremendous prestige and money, to bribe even a member of my crew. Waldron tried to sabotage our ship at the last hour, as you discovered."

"Will that be the end then?" Bruce asked, getting up and following his father to the open entryway of the ship.

"I am sure it won't," said Dr. Rhodes, going down onto the ground. "You can be certain they will try again and again."

Bruce followed him down and they started off to the charthouse nearby. "We'll stop them; we've got to stop them!"

They walked on. "It won't be easy," said his father at last. "They'll stop at nothing, not even at murder."

Bruce tightened his lips. "What is the price of five men's lives, including my own, if the lives of billions of people are at stake?"

Dr. Rhodes looked at his son, liked what he saw. "That's the way I look at it, son." He glanced at his watch. "We've got another forty minutes before take-off. Come on in and meet the rest of our crew."

As they approached the charthouse, the door popped open and a young fellow came out looking for them. He seemed rather upset, and when he saw Dr. Rhodes approaching, waved to him in relief. "I was just about to look for you," the man called.

"Something come up?" asked Dr. Rhodes.

The newcomer, Bruce saw, seemed to be in his early twenties. A wide-awake sort of chap, with sparkling dark eyes, and a shock of unruly black hair. Right now, he had grabbed the old engineer by the arm and was saying, "What's this about Waldron? He just phoned from the airport and says he's going to call the police. He said something about an attack on him and that he was going to have you all arrested!"

"What's that?" gasped Bruce and his father at the same time. And Bruce added, "He's lying! Waldron was trying to damage the ship!"

"Yes," Dr. Rhodes put in. "And he's still trying to hurt our flight. This is a new trick!"

At this point two other men, overhearing the excited words, came out of the little frame structure that held their charts and the machines by which their space course was being determined. One was a shortish man, with an olive complexion, and looking quite studious; the other tall and lanky, with thin blond hair and the deep-set eyes of an experienced space traveler.

The shorter man seemed alarmed by what he had heard. "If the police come, it will delay our take-off. If we delay beyond our limit, we will have to refigure everything all over again. It will be days before we can make a new start!"

"That's exactly what Waldron's game is," said Bruce's father. "He still hopes to damage our flight. He wants to make us as much trouble as possible."

"What's this all about?" asked the tall blond chap.

Bruce's father hastily told them what had happened, that Waldron had evidently been in the pay of Terraluna.

They nodded thoughtfully when he was through. "But then," said the young fellow they had first met, "we're going to be shorthanded. How can we get a replacement for Waldron in a hurry?"

Dr. Rhodes put a hand on Bruce's shoulder. "My son has volunteered to join us. He's a bit young, but I think he can do his share."

The three others looked at Bruce. Then the youngest snorted a bit. "He's only a kid! How can we take a chance?"

Bruce grew angry. "I'm sixteen and I'll bet I'm as strong as you are! You just watch me!"

"O.K., O.K.," said his father hastily, "no arguments now. We haven't the time. I'd better introduce you."

The young chap with the black hair turned out to be Arpad Benz, the other spacehand who would work with Bruce at the general jobs, engine room, manual and other chores aboard ship. He shook hands hesitantly.

The short Latin-appearing man was named Frank Garcia, and he was to be the ship's astrogator, the navigator of space. He had been an expert charter of astronomical courses for many years on the space lines to Mars and Venus and was considered one of the best.

The tall lanky man was their pilot, Kurt Jennings. He needed no further introduction to Bruce, who had heard of his exploits many times. Jennings was famous. He had pioneered a number of important flights, and had been the first to land on a couple of Jupiter's moons. Bruce knew his father was fortunate to have Jennings along, because if anybody could pilot this unusual trip, Jennings could.

Jennings said now, "If Waldron has called the police, they may be here in a half-hour. We've got to leave then or else we can't make it."

Garcia glanced at his watch. "Yes. As a matter of fact we have barely thirty minutes to get in the ship, get it on the rails, and start."

"Then let's go!" Dr. Rhodes said. "Hurry!"

Garcia dashed back into the charthouse and emerged a few minutes after with his arms loaded with lists and notebooks containing the figures for their course. He took these to the ship himself, to set up on the racks in the control room.

Jennings, Arpad and Bruce got aboard a little hand truck that stood nearby, drove rapidly down to the bunkhouse behind the chart structure and stopped. There the three of them rushed inside, grabbed the suitcases that had been packed that morning and other odds and ends not already aboard the ship. These they slammed on the truck and raced back to the ship.

Dr. Rhodes and Garcia were already inside. The truck that had been adding the last of their fuel had already backed off and started away.

Arpad and Bruce unloaded and rushed the stuff aboard ship. Bruce had some idea of the layout from his first visit. This helped to confirm his impressions.

In the rear of the long bullet-shaped craft were the rocket tubes, the fuel tanks, the engines, and other machinery, all except the tiny engine room, sealed off from the rest of the ship by sheets of special plastic that would not permit the passage of atomic rays. It was this plastic, which had been developed fifty years before, which alone permitted the use of atomic energy in such closed quarters as a space ship.

Along the center of the ship, above the engines, ran a narrow corridor. Along this corridor, on either side, were the tiny storage cabins, kitchen, sleeping quarters, and the airlock entrance.

At the end of the corridor, occupying the entire nose of the ship, was the control room. Two padded seats before the transparent nose were the places where the pilot and his relief would sit. Another similar chair just behind them for the astrogator, who sat before a panel of calculators built into the side.

Jennings and Dr. Rhodes were already in the first two seats. Dr. Rhodes was speaking on the communicator to the port crew outside, who were getting ready to haul the entire ship into place on the launching rack.

Garcia slid into his place. Arpad and Bruce got the last of the stuff loaded, and shut and sealed the airlock door.

Arpad motioned to Bruce. "You and I had better get ourselves into our launching hammocks without delay. You take the one on that side," he pointed, "and I'll take this one. Come along, I'll show you."

He hurried Bruce into the cabin nearest the airlock. There he lowered a deep padded hammock connected firmly from the sides of the small cabin.

"I know," said Bruce, not wanting Arpad to think him completely unfamiliar. "I made a vacation trip to the moon several years ago. I can handle this. You better hurry yourself."

Arpad nodded. "O.K. Don't forget to strap yourself in." He left on the run.

Bruce climbed into the hammock, pulled the straps about him. He saw that he faced a window by his side, and turning his head, he got a fairly good view of what was going on.

The ship had been resting on a sort of wide flatcar which was now being hooked up to a couple of squat atomic-engined land tugs. These huge tractor-like vehicles, once attached, then began to roll the space ship toward the mountain's base.

The ship vibrated gently as the wheels of the car turned. Finally it reached the beginning of the rack.

Running up the side of the mountain, a huge peak,

was a long track that was straight as an arrow. Great metal hoops ringed it in to make it a sort of skeleton tunnel bending upward until the top of it pointed directly into the sky like the barrel of some huge gun.

The flatcar jolted up against the end of the track. The land tugs now puffed around to each side of the ship and by means of huge buffer arms shoved the long space rocket off the wheeled base and into the level end of the launching rack.

Bruce could see most of this operation from his side porthole, through the thick unbreakable glassine substance that composed it. He knew what was going on and could imagine what he could not see.

The land tugs chugged away. Up front, Garcia called out, on the ship's internal phone system, "One minute more. Check your belts. Relax."

The phone system was left open. Bruce could hear their voices. Jennings was checking off the control-board readings with Dr. Rhodes. Then Dr. Rhodes said, "There's a car back at the charthouse coming our way. I see someone standing up in it waving at us."

"Yes," Jennings' voice said. "Looks like a police car. Probably want us to hold our take-off."

"Don't pay any attention, chief," said Garcia anxiously. "We've got thirty seconds."

"Ignore them," said Dr. Rhodes brusquely. "Twenty-five seconds."

They bent to their work. Bruce thought he heard

the faint sound of a siren in the distance. He imagined the police rushing to the end of the launching rack trying to prevent the take-off.

The time passed interminably now, with Garcia again calling off the seconds. Then finally came the five-second call, then four, three, two, one, off!

The ship vibrated easily. At that instant, Jennings had thrown in the first jet, a small thrust capable only of moving the ship a little along the tracks. This was enough to start the automatic magnetic reaction.

The tracks led upward through hoops that were magnetically activated. Once a space ship started in motion at the end of the track, each hoop picked up the metal cylindrical body and thrust it further along. Attraction from ahead, repulsion from the hoops they passed, and the ship was thrust faster and faster along the rails.

Once started, the process could not be stopped. As the ship began its slide upward, Bruce felt the first effects of acceleration. His hammock began to slide down and the cabin tilted steadily as the ship began to nose upward along the tracks.

Now faster and faster Bruce saw the hoops flash by his porthole. Jennings turned on more jets, adding to the speed of the vessel's passage.

The rocket ship sped along the launching-rack slide with ever greater speed. Now it was angling almost straight up and from the control-room seats the open blue-sky end of the magnetic tunnel came into sight and enlarged rapidly.

With steadily increasing momentum the great metal

bullet raced upward, streams of atomic fire now blasting from its rear. Bruce felt himself being pushed
down more and more into the padding of his hammock. He felt as if a great hand was shoving down
on his chest.

Then like a bullet from a gun the ship shot out
of the end of the half-mile long rack, and Jennings
slammed in the full force of its engines.

There was a moment of intolerable pressure. Bruce
felt as if he were strangling, as if an invisible ele-
phant had suddenly sat down on him, crushing him
deep into the padding. He gasped for breath, fought
to keep himself from blacking out.

For instant after instant he seemed about to be
crushed completely. He caught glimpses out of the
corner of his tortured eye of the porthole getting
darker and darker, of the blue merging into blackness.

Then, at last, as he began to feel that he could
bear the strain no longer, as if he would sink into
total unconsciousness, the terrible pressure ceased.
There was a moment of intense relief and he found
himself fighting to control his pumping lungs.

Bruce knew then that the ship was free of Earth's
grip; it was on its way!

Chapter 3 The Other Side of the Moon

As soon as Bruce had unstrapped himself from his hammock, he found himself in the state of "free-fall" that is so familiar to space fliers. Bruce discovered that there was nothing at all pleasing about having no weight, in spite of the fascination this no-gravity condition seems to hold for those who have never been in space. He felt as if he were going to be sick, as if his stomach were jumping, and his eyes and ears straining to detect something which wasn't there. It was the same sort of sensation that he would have had had he been falling from the top of a very high building and had not yet hit the ground.

It took a little time to readjust himself to this strange feeling. He had to think about his every

motion rather consciously for the first few hours, for
when he did not, his muscles, expecting through habit
to find the resistance of weight, would strike out force-
fully and then wildly in sudden panic. The uneasiness of the falling feeling was always there, and it
took concentration to build up the new set of mental
commands for his body to act by.

Bruce was not entirely unfamiliar with the feeling.
When he'd paid the visit to his father at the Copernicus research base, he'd gone through all these sensa-
tions before. Although he had tried to steel himself
for what was coming, it was still alarming when it
came.

Fortunately, perhaps, he did not have time to sit
around and worry about his feelings. In the few hours
that the moon hop would take, there was work to
be done. Arpad Benz was already in the central corridor, swinging from the various straps and stanchions
that were the means of motion in the floating interior
of the ship. "Come on, Bruce," he called. "Now's the
time to pitch in. We've got to get the moon-runners
unfolded and set up."

Bruce reached for a leather strap that hung from
the wall nearby and, using it as Tarzan in the movies
once used the branches of trees, swung himself after
Arpad. He knew what the moon-runners were, but
he had never quite realized that it was necessary to
go outside the ship to adjust them. The young spaceman who had guyed him originally was now climbing
into a pressurized space suit.

Bruce wasn't sure what he would have to do, but

he had made up his mind that there was nothing anyone could do that he could not do also. He was ready for anything. Let Arpad kid him about his age, let the others think what they would, they would find that he was up to the job.

Arpad helped him into the space suit, zipped up the pressure-tight fabric coverall, fitted the transparent plastic helmet, and checked the heating and air regulators. The helmet phone on, Arpad explained what they had to do while they stood in the little space lock as the ship's air was pumped out.

When the outer hull door swung open, Bruce gazed down into the blackness of outer space. Covering half the view was the glowing surface of the Earth, a gorgeous and awe-inspiring hemisphere, like a relief map in school, save for the breath-taking depth and color. The soft greens and deep blues of field and ocean, the blinding white of the poles, all merged into each other. Over all the misty masses of clouds and humid air belts, a creeping twilight purple zone along one rim drifted slowly. Bruce stared, forgetting for the moment the bottomless gap that hung between the tiny bulk of their ship and his home world.

"Come on, come on," said Arpad's voice, "no time for daydreaming, we've got work to do!" Bruce snapped out of it, turned, and followed Arpad along the outer surface of the ship, the magnetic gloves and shoes of his space suit sticking to the outer hull just as a fly sticks to a ceiling.

The moon-runners were in the form of long ridges

that Bruce had at first taken for part of the ship's
streamlining. Now he saw that they were really hard-
metal runners, the length of the ship, which could
be cranked outward from their snug contact to extend
into two parallel runners just like the runners of a
sled or a pair of skis. Though they would have been
very heavy on Earth, here in weightlessness Bruce
and Arpad were able to crank them away from the
hull by hand, snap their bracing girders into place,
and thus clear the ship for its lunar landing.

When the job was done, Arpad and Bruce worked
their way back to the lock, returned inside, and took
off their space suits. It had not occurred to Bruce
that this ship would be landed in the way most com-
mercial and explorer craft used, rather than in the
fancy tail-jet acrobatics plus magnetic absorbers
which were in use on the elaborate passenger liners.
He rather looked forward to the experience. As he
made his way to the front of the ship, he realized
that the craft was laid out as an airplane would be,
to be flown from front to back and not from top to
bottom.

Arpad announced as they entered the control room,
"Runners all set, Doc. Shall we secure the gear?"

Dr. Rhodes, Jennings, and Garcia were all present
there. Rhodes and Garcia were at the calculating
machines, working on their course. Jennings was in
the pilot seat, watching the engines and the oncoming features of the moon.

Over Jennings' shoulder, Bruce saw that the white
and gray features of our satellite were looming large,

showing the sharp and cold barrenness familiar to
telescope observers. It was a scene that disturbed
him by its lack of warmth, by the intensity of its
harsh shadows and dazzling white spaces. Now, without any atmosphere to blur the vision and approaching it at speeds of many miles a second, it took his
breath away.

"Yes," Bruce's father raised his head from his work,
"you'd better see that nothing was damaged by the
take-off. We shall be landing at the mining base by
the Einstein Sea to take on our final fuel load. I don't
want to stay there any longer than is absolutely
necessary."

Garcia looked up at them briefly, grunted. Jennings,
at the controls, shook his head slightly as if uneasy
at the prospect. Bruce noticed these reactions and,
as he and Arpad went out, he glanced at his fellow
spaceman in wonder.

But for once Arpad was silent, a thoughtful look
on his face. Without conversation, they went through
each chamber and locker checking the contents and
testing the straps and locks. As they were buckling
down a box that held a small stock of weapons and
ammunition, Bruce finally broke the silence:

"Is something wrong? What's the worry?"

Arpad hesitated a moment. "Well, it's going to be
kind of risky to land there. After all, that is one of
Terraluna's main bases. They'll have to fuel us, because that's UN orders, but you can just bet they're
going to try to think up some way of making trouble

for us, maybe cripple the ship. It's going to be very
risky to stay there long."

"Then why don't we land somewhere else—say at
the regular UN Commission post near Mare Crisium?"
Bruce suggested.

"Uh-uh," Arpad shook his head. "That's on the
Earth side of the moon. We've got to make our take-
off from the outer side of the moon in order to avoid
the extra complications of Earth's gravity. The only
good bases on that side are the mining company's.
So that's where we've got to go."

Bruce tightened his lips as they continued. He'd
never been on the far side of the moon, the side
that was never seen from Earth, but he knew that
it was almost like another nation, so extensive were
the Terraluna holdings and control there. If something underhanded happened to them there, some
"accident," there would be no one to help them or
to get them justice. It was going to be up to them to
be on the alert.

Their landing time came soon enough, though it
was actually a number of hours more. In that period
the ship had been reversed and jets applied for the
purpose of bringing the ship down to a safe speed
for landing. To land a ship flat on runners, it is necessary first to circle the planet two or three times in
order to brake the speed, to bring it down to something low enough to be controlled like an airplane
on the Earth. Space speeds are so great that in order
to do this it is necessary to allow the craft to swing

about the planet in a narrowing orbit, coming nearer and nearer the surface as it slows. Its speed in relation to that of the planetary surface had to be made nearly equal.

Bruce found that it took almost the same length of time to slow down in this way as it had taken them to cross the distance from the Earth. During all that period, he and Arpad were standing ready for emergencies, as Jennings skilfully guided the craft over the face of Luna.

Bruce had a wonderful opportunity then to look at both the hemispheres of the moon, the one we know and the one Earth never sees. Both sides were very similar. On the outer side there were also the same type of flat, wide craters, of dry sea bottoms, and sharp high mountains. It had not been until after the first space explorers had circled the satellite that these features had been given names, generally those of the great pioneers of science and government of the last century.

Finally the ship was skimming low over the surface, passing over a last mountain range, and down over the wide, flat surface of the great Einstein Sea. This "sea," like all the others so called, was actually a vast, flat, dry plain. The mining base was tucked away in one corner near the jagged wall of a small deep crater.

Jennings brought the ship down lightly until they seemed to be skimming the surface. Then lower bit by bit until finally the runners touched and a sharp whistling vibration went through the space ship. They bounced a couple of times and finally went skiing over the surface like a toboggan over snow. For the sea was a sea in one sense—a sea of dust.

For millions of years cosmic dust had slowly settled over the airless surface of the moon. Its flat plains were layered with a thick coating of extremely fine dust, dozens of feet deep. It made an excellent landing spot for a ski-equipped ship. Their runners served the purpose.

Now they were skidding over the surface, a spray of dust finer than snow thrown up behind them that fell back again slowly onto the surface without leaving a cloud. Bruce was puzzled for a moment until he realized that without air there could be nothing to hold this dust up to make a cloud. It had to fall back immediately. Had this been on Earth, their dust spray might have hung in the air for hours.

Stationed at one side port, Bruce watched for the unexpected dangers or tilts, while Arpad watched from the opposite side. Jennings jockeyed the ship sliding toward the domes of the mining base.

Neatly the craft slid, with a last puff of its jets, through the huge gates of the hangar-dome and onto its smooth runway. The great doors slid shut, and they heard the throbbing of the pumps as the dome-enclosed hangar pumped air back. When the pressure was normal outside, Arpad unbolted the outer lock.

"Wait a minute, everyone," called Dr. Rhodes. He was hurrying down the corridor of the ship, followed by Jennings and Garcia. "Don't go out until you hear my instructions."

Bruce pulled down a wall-seat and sat down. He realized suddenly that he had weight again, even though it was much less than at home. Arpad grinned at him, "Tired?" Bruce realized that he was actually quite tired, but in the weightlessness of space, he simply hadn't noticed it. But he shook his head, determined not to let on.

Rhodes reached the port, and the others gathered around. For a moment he hesitated, then said slowly:

"I don't want anyone to leave this ship except on business. I want you all to be very, very cautious, to watch everything very carefully. Terraluna will certainly try again to stop us from making this trip. We are going to take on our final fuel load from their stores, and they are going to do this under UN orders. I don't know how, but I am sure that in some way they will attempt to damage this ship or prevent our success.

"Arpad, will you break out that case of guns and arm yourself and Bruce. I want you two to stand guard at all times outside this ship. Allow no one to enter it. Allow no one near it except those engaged in the fueling operation. I expect this to take no more than an hour and I intend to leave immediately afterward. Garcia and I still have some calculations to make on our asteroid hops, and I want Jennings to check the engines. That leaves it up to you two to see that we fuel all right and no one gets a chance to do us dirt."

In a few minutes more, Bruce and Arpad opened the hull door and emerged onto the floor of the hangar. As he set foot on the moon's surface, Bruce felt his heart pounding with a strange feeling of excitement and danger, his weariness forgotten. Around his waist was slung a thick leather belt, set with bullets and a bulky glistening machine-pistol swung in a holster at his side. His hand rested gently on the palm-fitting rubberized grip as he strode to where a group of workmen in Terraluna's blue overalls were wheeling over plastic drums of atomic fuel.

Chapter 4 Fuel for Fools

THE space-ship hangar was a huge enclosed metal bubble large enough to house several ships and leading into a series of similar metal bubbles housing the homes and workings of the mining enterprise. The ground was hard-packed lunar slate and the lighting came from giant atomic bulbs built into the tops of the domes, bulbs which once activated would not burn out for a thousand years. The air and heat were all artificially supplied and regulated. Outside these domes, life could not live for the airlessness of the moon and its weeks-long day made for terrible degrees of cold and heat, neither extreme of which would be tolerable for even an instant. Everything here was man-made and had been transported from Earth piece by piece.

Bruce reflected on this as he watched the fuel drums

being rolled out. Even though Terraluna was now bent on a project which might well be the ruin of all that man had built up over a million painful years of struggle, he could understand their desire to complete the mastery of this alien world. For a moment he almost forgot the danger of their visit until the harsh voice of one of the workmen brought him back to Earth—or rather to moon.

"You the guys getting this special speedy order, kid?"

For an instant Bruce flushed angrily. He knew he was young for a spaceman, but he doubted that he was any less the equal of these men. He fought back the angry retort that came to his lips, realizing in time that nothing nasty had been intended by the questioner.

"Yes," he replied quietly, "we're the ones. Take it around to the rear and run it into Tanks Four, Five, and Six." He gestured with one hand and stood back.

"Don't let them get you riled," said Arpad, coming up to him from the ship. "Keep your eye peeled." He waved a hand and walked around the ship to check it for flaws, for pitmarks that might have been caused by tiny meteors or cosmic particles.

Bruce walked slowly back and forth, warily watching the loading. There seemed to be nothing going wrong. The tanks were coming out of a connected dome whose entry door was plainly marked: *Fuel—Keep Out—Danger*. The fuel drums were all sealed and bore the standard markings of the United Nations Atomic Fuel Commission. Besides the workmen, no strangers were near them, though there were a couple of men watching from a doorway across the hangar.

Arpad came into sight again and caught Bruce's eye. The young spaceman waved a hand. "We made a pretty clean trip this time, only one little meteor scratch. Wanta see?"

"Sure," Bruce replied. "Where is it?"

"Around here," Arpad answered, taking his arm and leading him to the nose of the ship. He pointed out a thin scratch running diagonally for a couple of feet across the gleaming surface of the round nose of their vessel just beneath the transparent observation ports. "A small one grazed us. This is superhard metal so you can guess at what a speed this little pebble was traveling to even scratch it."

Bruce looked at the mark with interest. He thought of what might happen if a really big one got through their radar screens, and while he was thinking this, his ears registered something slightly different from the trudging and rumbling of the workmen and their hand trucks.

He turned and for a moment saw only one of the workmen wheeling the last drum of their fuel up to the loading vent. But this man was not alone, he was accompanied by three other individuals who were not in the regulation blue overalls. One of them, a short, plump, balding man, was wearing civilian gray moon-jumpers and was carrying a leather brief case. The two others were hard-faced, soldierly looking men, in Terraluna guard blues, wearing belts to which holstered weapons were attached.

Instantly Bruce turned and walked rapidly up to them. The workman went on about his job, but the three others started toward the airlock entrance. Bruce called out to them:

"Wait just a moment, please! Nobody is allowed in the ship!"

The three paid him little attention, dismissing him with a glance, hastening their steps. Bruce made a dash for the entry, gained it a few steps ahead of them and blocked the door. "Hold it! If you have any business with this ship, tell me and I'll have someone come out, but I can't let you in."

The short puffy man stopped short, turned red. One of the armed men, however, came ahead, scowling. "Go on, fellow, and don't block us. We've got to see the captain and we're going in."

He tried to brush Bruce away with his hand. Almost without thinking, Bruce darted his hand to his belt and drew out his machine-pistol. He thrust its muzzle to within a few inches of the man's body. "Stand back!" he snapped.

Taken by surprise, the three stepped back quickly; and the two in blue reached for their own weapons. Bruce raised his gun, tightened his grip. "Don't try anything," he said. "I have my orders. You can have no legitimate business aboard this ship!"

The little man in gray regained his composure and waved his companions back. He spoke to Bruce impatiently, "But we certainly do have business here. I happen to be the UN's official agent at this base. It is my duty to certify all ships reaching this port before

they leave. I shall have to examine this craft in person
before I can give that permission. So let us in at once
and let us get on with our affairs!"

Bruce shook his head stubbornly. "I can't let you
in, regardless of what you say. This ship is a UN ship
itself and on business for the UN. You can check that
with Copernicus by radio. In fact, you must know that
already because you got orders to fuel us."

The official grew red-faced again. "I don't care what
Copernicus may say. How do I know this is actually
the ship it claims to be? My orders are that no ship
may leave here without being certified. If you do not
instantly put that ugly gun down and stand aside, I
shall see that you do not leave here at all!"

He started forward as if to brave his way through,
but Bruce thrust a hand across the entry and kept his
gun leveled. "Come a step farther and I will shoot!"

His heart was beating fast. He didn't know what
would happen if he had to make good his threat, but
he remembered only one thing. He could not permit
these men aboard the ship. It was obvious that the
official's claim was merely a trick. Probably he wasn't
even a UN representative. Legal or not, whatever it
was, was just a means to Terraluna's efforts to stop
the expedition.

Evidently the men realized that Bruce was not
bluffing, for they stepped away and drew back. Arpad,
who had been watching with amazement, stepped up
beside Bruce and whispered, "I'll get the chief." He
went into the ship.

For a while Bruce blocked the door in silence. The

three men were whispering among themselves. Several of the workmen were standing near the domes watching the events in silence.

Dr. Rhodes came to the portway. "What's all this about?" he said.

The puffy official came back to the ship and explained what he had told Bruce before. Dr. Rhodes frowned and shook his head. "No, I cannot permit you aboard this ship. I was informed that the United Nations had radioed advance clearance for this ship and priority. This should be sufficient for your certification."

The little man went back and whispered some more to his Terraluna companions. He looked back to Dr. Rhodes. "As the official agent of the UN here, I refuse to grant you clearance. Until you allow my inspection, you are denied permission to leave this base." He turned to the men in blue. "I charge you to see that they obey my orders!" He then stalked away and disappeared into one of the domes, as if whatever followed would no longer concern him.

Dr. Rhodes looked after him silently, then he turned to Bruce. "Did they complete the fueling?" When Bruce nodded, he added, "Come inside."

The engineer stepped back into the airlock, followed by his son, who closed the outer door and began to bolt it. Dr. Rhodes gained the central corridor and called out, "Everybody get to take-off stations! We are leaving immediately!"

Bruce hastily slammed the inner airlock door and began to seal its rubberoid fastenings. Arpad was already running down to the engine room, while Dr. Rhodes rushed back to the control room.

Bruce heard Garcia's excited protest, "But our figuring is not completed yet!"

"Never mind that!" shouted Dr. Rhodes. "We'll finish it in space. Jennings, get her started! We've not a second to lose!"

Bruce got the last seals shut. Outside he heard the muffled shouts of men and someone began pounding on the side. He heard a voice call out:

"You can't take off! You have no permission! We'll blast you as an outlaw if you don't open up at once!"

He glanced forward along the central corridor. He could see Jennings already in his control seat, Rhodes and Garcia beside him.

By a side port, Bruce saw the men outside run away from the ship as Jennings signaled their intentions. A single blast of their smallest jet made everyone in the hangar run for cover. The ship swung around, faced the great gates of the hangar. Bruce heard Jennings' voice boom out on their radio speaker:

"Get those gates open or we'll blast through them without waiting!"

The ship's engines were rumbling away. Another puff of rocket energy and the ship swung slowly forward on its runners. In the nick of time, the gates started sliding back. The remaining air in the hangar dome puffed out, but the Terraluna base operators had all gotten safely under cover.

The ship slid through the gates, slid out onto the vast expanse of the gray dust sea, which stretched

before them as a plain that reached to the horizon,
where Bruce could see the white sunlit tops of the
jagged lunar mountains that ringed it in.

The ship jockeyed slowly into position. Behind
them, at the hangar, Bruce now saw several men come
out, dressed in bulky red and yellow space suits. He
caught a glimpse of something bright and shinily
metallic being rolled out before them.

"They'll stop at nothing," he heard his father say,
"they can't afford not to. They mean murder!"

As their ship gathered speed, its runners moving
smoothly over the thick velvety surface, the radio an-
nouncer in their control room boomed with a strange
voice:

"Stop that ship or we'll fire! This is the port com-
mander ordering!"

"Go ahead," said Dr. Rhodes to Jennings. "Full
speed and up!"

The ship's rockets blasted out in full. As they pulled
rapidly away from the domes of the mining camp,
Bruce saw a puff of yellow flash from the tiny figures
outside. There was an explosion somewhere behind
them. They were being fired at!

But it was too late. The Rhodes' expedition skimmed
along faster and faster, its runners gliding over the
sea bottom. Then easily and gently it lifted up, shot
into the black sky, skimmed the jagged tops of the
mountains and tore onward into the interplanetary
void.

Behind them Bruce saw the mining camp quickly
diminish into a group of tiny gleaming bubbles, then

into a speck on the edge of a flat grayish plain, then vanish against the face of the moon. He saw the moon itself pull together, shrinking until it became a single disk against the black sky, and then finally there was the breath-taking vision of two disks, the softly glowing green and blue Earth and partly blotting it out the black and white harshly outlined features of its dead satellite.

They were off at last with Saturn eight hundred million miles away!

Chapter 5 Cosmic Hitchhike

"HEY, snap out of it!" Arpad's voice cut into Bruce's thoughts as he stood staring back at the receding moon. "There's work to be done; no time for sight-seeing now."

Bruce reluctantly took his eyes off the breath-taking sight of the dual planet of his birth and brought his attention back to the present. Arpad was already at work picking up some papers and stuff that had become loose in the unexpected take-off. Without being told further, Bruce joined him and checked the cargo again. Fortunately, not very much had been unfastened during their brief call at Luna, and so the sudden dash away had not created the havoc that it ordinarily would have.

Again, the fact that their take-off was from a small

47

body had not involved the intense pressures and speeds
that their original breakaway from Earth had de-
manded. The smaller the planet, the easier it is for a
rocket to break away from its gravitational grip. This
was an old story; every schoolboy in Bruce's time
knew it.

Jennings came back down the corridor and waved
to the two spacehands. "Drop what you're doing.
We've got a job that's more important!"

When they made their way to him, Jennings said:
"Dr. Rhodes thinks there's a chance the ship was
hit by one of those shots. I don't think so myself, but
we don't dare overlook it. One of you will have to
get into a space suit and check the outside hull
carefully."

"I'll do it," Bruce exclaimed just a second before
Arpad could offer. The other shrugged his shoulders,
stepped back.

"O.K.," Jennings nodded, "but don't waste any time
about it."

Bruce went to the airlock, got into the space suit
just as he had before when they were attaching the
landing runners, and, controlling the lock's air pressure, let himself out. Again he felt the frightening
feeling of immense height, of being suspended over a
bottomless hole in which two immense balls were
floating and a number of brilliant pin-point stars
peering up from the infinite depths.

Concentrating his gaze on the shining metal outer
surface of the ship, being careful to keep his magnetic
shoes firmly flat against the side, and his safety line

clear of snags, Bruce crawled slowly over the ship's outside.

From pointed top to blunt and tube-studded end, along its vanes and runners, Bruce checked minutely. But there was no sign of any of the Terraluna shells having hit the ship. He was glad, some time later, to be able to make his way back to the airlock and return to the safety of the interior. By this time, he observed as he closed the outer door of the lock that the Earth-Moon globes had receded noticeably.

No sooner had he returned to the interior, and the automatic buzzer that always accompanied the operation of the airlock had quieted, than the atomic jets blasted again, and Bruce felt himself gaining an apparent weight as the ship moved forward in a new acceleration.

Another buzzer indicated that everyone was wanted in the control room. Bruce, having taken his space suit off and hung it away, made his way forward, clumsily stumbling against the force of the ship's blasts.

In the control room, at the front of the ship, Jennings was seated in the pilot's chair, watching the movement of the dials that recorded the operation of the engines and the direction of the ship. Guided by a series of notations and figures that had been produced by Garcia's navigational calculations and planet charts, he moved a dial every now and then to check and regulate the enormous energies being liberated into space by the disintegration of their atomic rocket fuel.

Garcia was still punching out figures on his calculating machines, apparently checking his information again. Dr. Rhodes was holding a star chart and studying it.

Arpad was already in the room, and when Bruce came in, all looked up. Dr. Rhodes glanced briefly at his son, smiled, then became serious. He addressed them all:

"Our unexpected departure from the refueling base has made it necessary to refigure our course and replot our charts. We are now a few hours ahead of our plans and facing in a slightly different direction than we had expected. We are therefore swinging the ship around and going faster in order to try to catch our first scheduled stop. We'll be moving under jet blasts off and on for the next few hours as a result."

The others nodded. Bruce was puzzled, and as he realized that his father was engaged in explaining everything for the mutual benefit of all, he felt it only right to express his puzzlement.

"I don't quite understand, Dad," he said, "what you mean by stops. Aren't we going directly to Saturn? Wouldn't that be the speediest and straightest course?"

His father nodded. "That would be the speediest and most direct way to go, if it were possible to do it that way. Unfortunately, it is not. We do not possess either the energy or the type of engine to make such a trip. Neither, I must add, does any other space ship ever made. It might be possible to make one, but it would be so big and expensive that no one would see any use for it. You see, the trip to Saturn is tremendously farther than any space ship has ever gone before. Not only that, but speaking in terms of the sun and the solar system that revolves around it, it would be an all uphill trip."

He paused for a moment, then waved a hand. "Gather around this chart."

Arpad and Bruce looked at the map which showed the various bodies of the sun's system. Dr. Rhodes explained:

"As you know, a space ship does not travel directly to its planetary destination. Instead, to save fuel, it establishes its own closed orbit around the sun, but in such a way and at such a speed that sooner or later it will happen to cross the orbit of its goal at the same time that the goal is there. In other words, if we head for Mars, we ignore where Mars is when we take off, but head for the spot in space where it will be when we reach that spot."

"You mean," Bruce put in, "something like making a date to meet a friend at a place where you and he both must travel to get to."

"That's the idea," said his father. "And since we can't ask the planet to go some special way, we have to do all the planning to be where the planet will be going."

"Well, then," said Bruce, "aren't we simply going to find out where Saturn will be and go there directly?"

"No," was the engineer's answer, "because that would require traveling all that far way against the pull of the sun. Such an orbit would require immense amounts of energy to establish, because instead of merely breaking away from the pull of the Earth, which is hard enough as you know, we would have to fight all the way against the pull of the sun itself. Saturn is farther away from the sun than the Earth, eight hundred million miles farther, since our home planet is only ninety-two million miles 'upward' from the sun. This is a pull which would require blasting all the way and no ship could carry that amount of fuel.

"So what we are going to do is to hitchhike our way!"

"Whaaat!" said Arpad incredulously. "How can you do that?"

Garcia, who had stopped his work at last, smiled, looked up. "We'll thumb a ride on the asteroids."

Rhodes nodded. "Exactly. It so happens that the tiny little planets called asteroids that mostly revolve between Mars and Jupiter give us our steppingstones. There are thousands of these little worlds and some of them, fortunately for us, have very wild orbits."

"Yes, that's right," said Bruce excitedly, "some of them come close to the Earth, too. There's Eros and Amor and Adonis—they all come to a few million miles of the Earth."

Rhodes nodded. "There are asteroids that go clear inward to the orbit of Venus, nearer the sun than ourselves. And what interests us more, there are some that go out way beyond even Jupiter. One especially, named Hidalgo, goes almost out to the orbit of Saturn itself."

"Then are we going to Hidalgo?"

"Not directly, that's impossible," said Rhodes, "but

that will be our final hitching post. Hidalgo happens right now to be passing the orbit of Jupiter and to be heading almost directly for Saturn. If we can catch it in time, we can simply ride it almost all the rest of the way.

"But we're not even going to go there directly. We're going to pick up a near asteroid first, one near the Earth that's heading outward. We'll ride it beyond the orbit of Mars, where we'll jump off it and jump onto another asteroid that will take us most of the way through the asteroid belt. Then we'll leave that one for another that will take us near Hidalgo, where we can make our landing. We'll settle down on Hidalgo for a few weeks until we are close to Saturn, and then we'll make our final leap to our real objective."

"Wow!" said Arpad, while Bruce whistled.

"It took plenty of figuring," said Garcia, shaking his head over his machines. "Plenty. We had to work out the orbits of dozens and dozens of these little worldlets. We had to figure speeds and directions and timing. That's why we're wasting fuel now trying to get back to where we should have been if we had followed our original calculations. Otherwise the new figures will be terribly difficult."

"Then, actually we won't do too much flying, only short hops between asteroids, letting their own orbital force carry us along against the sun's pull," contributed Bruce again, studying the chart with its circles tangled in each other like the web of a drunken spider.

"Correct," said Rhodes.

At that moment Jennings called out, "Apollo is in sight, sir!"

Rhodes sprang to the viewing port. Bruce could see nothing save the usual mass of stars and lights, but evidently the trained eye of the pilot had spotted a new one. The engineer squinted a minute, looked up. "To stations!" he called.

Bruce and Arpad dashed back to the posts that had been assigned them on such occasions. Arpad was stationed near the engines to watch for any trouble. Bruce was located by the airlock to be able to take any necessary steps that an emergency might call for. Fortunately for him, it was also located near a port from which he could see most of what was going on.

He felt the ship changing course as the gyroscopic controls swung it about. He felt a series of jets blast against the body of the vessel as it worked in for a landing.

Now he could see the tiny disk of white which was the oncoming asteroid. Apollo was a very tiny one, he knew, but one of those that came close to Earth's orbit. It swung back and forth in his view as the ship switched in toward it.

Gradually it assumed shape, and he saw to his surprise that it was not a sphere as he had always assumed planetary bodies to be. Instead, it seemed to be a huge chunk of rock, irregular in shape, rather like a big boulder, longer on one side than on the other, and slowly swinging end over end on itself.

For a moment Bruce was puzzled until he remembered his school studies in astronomy. He realized then that Apollo could not be more than a few miles wide, and its own internal gravity therefore much too weak to pull it into a spherical shape when it was originally formed, hot and molten. It had cooled off too quickly to become anything more than an irregular mass of barren rock.

Landing on Apollo was tricky as a result. It was not a question of skimming in on a smooth surface. Rather it was a swinging about, gauging the weird swing of its sharp edges, dodging under one huge overhanging jagged end and swooping down into a valley scooped out of one side.

It took a couple of hours for the dodging and twisting landing to be made, during all of which time Bruce was glued breathlessly to the port, watching the mass of gleaming gray and white streaked rock fill the view, move suddenly into them as if they were going to fall violently against it, suddenly swing away with dizzying speed, then level off, shift again and again. It was like watching a landscape go mad as the dwarfed space ship edged up against the free-moving mass of rock, a mass probably not larger than the Island of Manhattan, yet a world of its own. And then the Apollo landscape leveled off and the ship touched surface with unexpected gentleness, and stopped.

They had made their first hitchhike safely.

Chapter 6 Tampered Charts

APOLLO was a strange place. When everything had been made shipshape, Jennings and Bruce were given leave to go outside and explore the little world. Their trip would not be just for fun; there were very practical reasons.

For one thing, as Dr. Rhodes explained to everyone shortly after their landing, there was a very specific and limited length of time which they would stay. Apollo was moving outward toward the orbit of Mars. At a certain point it would come within a few hundred thousand miles of another asteroid. This asteroid would be at its own nearest point to the sun. They would then transfer there, ride that body out almost to Jupiter's orbit and finally be able to leap to Hidalgo.

Bruce asked if Mars would be near them at any

time, but Garcia shook his head. The navigator said, "Mars happens to be on the other side of the sun at the moment. We may pass its orbit, but if we wanted to meet Mars we'd have a wait of more than a year before it came around to where we'd be."

"But what would happen if we failed to make one of our jumps on time?" Bruce then asked.

There was a silence for a few minutes. Garcia frowned. "It would be very serious. We'd have to figure where next best to leap, or else make a very wide jump on our own. The latter would cut into our fuel more heavily than we could afford. Either course would compel us to spend an awful long time on new calculations. Time is what we cannot afford."

So when Bruce and Jennings stepped out, suitably protected in their space clothes, it was mainly for the purpose of observing the little worldlet's motion in space and the apparent movements of the stars and planets in the jet-black airless sky. There would be need of making astronomical observations to check their position and these could not be made without first determining the tricks of sky as seen from Apollo.

The effect was strange. Bruce felt almost as weightless standing outside the ship as he had in deep space. The little asteroid was so tiny that his weight would be measured in ounces only. With his Earth muscles capable of carrying many pounds, he had to be extremely careful when he moved. A normal step might cause him to fly up hundreds of feet, to drift slowly down far from where he took off. He did this the first time he tried to walk, and it was an eerie experience.

From where he floated helpless, drifting like a feather very gently downward, he could see the surface of the asteroid. It was all rocky, unrelieved by either water or air or soil. Its edges were sharp and harsh. The light of sun and stars glinted brilliantly in spots and where there were shadows, they were utterly dark.

As he drifted down, he could see Jennings standing by the side of the space ship waving to him. The pilot was hanging on to the rocky surface with a long hook. In addition, he had tied a long rope to himself running to the ship. He was holding another end for Bruce to fasten, and had been about to give it to Bruce when the boy's thoughtless first step had sent him into the sky.

Bruce caught his breath and waited. Eventually, minutes later, he floated to the surface, and Jennings drifted over to him and attached the rope to a ring in the space-suit's belt.

"Must have gotten a real scare, eh?" said Jennings on their helmet phones.

"Well," said Bruce, "it was a surprise for sure."

"Look up," said the pilot, pointing. Bruce gazed with him up at the sky.

It was brilliant and wonderful and quite unusual. Instead of the blue of Earth, the sky was as black as if seen from a space ship. The stars and planets seemed also as if seen from space, but they were moving. The whole sky was slowly turning. It made Bruce quite dizzy to watch it for any length of time.

"Apollo is revolving rather rapidly, which is not

surprising in a world of this size," said Jennings. "We've got to calculate just how fast and in what way it is turning, so that we can figure out just which stars we are seeing and when we can expect to spot the various bodies we will be guided by."

They set up automatic cameras which would snap sky pictures regularly over several hours. These would then be studied and used as the basis for Garcia's calculations. They set up telescopes for identifying rapidly the various bodies, and in a fairly short time they had solved the basic part of their problems.

Bruce looked about him from time to time. Because the worldlet was not spherical but almost oblong, and their position was in a rather hollowed-out valley near the line of its axis, the effect was almost frightening. Instead of a horizon, they seemed to be camped between two incredibly tremendous mountains—for each pole of the tiny planet loomed before them like a mountain many miles high.

As the days passed, and the routine of remapping their charts neared completion, Bruce had a couple of occasions to go exploring out to the ends of the asteroid. He discovered to his astonishment that the apparent mountains seemed to lie down as he approached them. For their effect of towering was a gravitational trick. As he walked along the flat ground, the mountains would lean farther and farther down away from him. But when he would look back, he would get the equally horrifying effect of seeming to be gazing down a steep precipice. All about would be the sharp edges of the black sky, the hard cold rock, the slowly whirling sky and the shifting madness of the view as seen from the ground.

Then one day he was out near the ragged end of the asteroid. Several hundred yards before him he knew the ground fell away into a bottomless cliff. He anchored himself carefully to an outcropping of rock, and pulled out a set of the newly revised sky charts. With a pocket telescope adjustment that he could attach to the eye frame of his space-suit helmet he set out to identify the planetary bodies visible. This end of the asteroid happened at the moment to be facing front in Apollo's course outward. It was a little like riding the prow of a ship.

There were several disks in the black sky, discernible as planets rather than the far-off stars. Saturn was visible, its rings noticeable even at that distance. Jupiter was out of sight and so was Mars. One disk could be identified as Uranus, out beyond Saturn.

But the several other observable disks were all asteroids—for they were approaching the rim of the asteroid belt.

Bruce focused on a bright one and with a little mental figuring determined it to be Juno, one of the largest asteroids, one of the very first ever to have been discovered by man. He picked another bright one and studied it.

He became puzzled. He checked his chart, but the body in the sky did not seem to correspond with any given there. Something was wrong. Bruce knew that a body so visible should be marked on their charts—after all, he and Jennings and Garcia and

even Arpad had worked on these sky maps the past
few days.

He studied the body again, noticing its evidence
of motion in relation to the other bodies, especially
to Juno. He saw that it was near Apollo, very near. He
saw that it would pass them quite closely. And he
knew that there was only one asteroid that was due to
pass them that closely. That was the asteroid that was
to be their next landing spot!

Bruce was electrified. This was all wrong! The chart
was wrong, it was off by a couple of days. Yet on it,
the other bodies were correct. Just this one asteroid,
this most important of all asteroids, was misplaced on
his chart.

If he had guessed right, they would have to take off
almost at once to make their leap in time. And nobody
back at the ship would be ready!

He detached himself from the rock, heart pounding.
He started back to the ship, several miles away, trying
to call on his helmet radio. But the ship could not
hear him, for between Bruce and it was half an asteroid
of rock, and there was no atmospheric layer in the sky
to bounce a message down.

Bruce leaped and floated dangerously along, breath-
less, desperate. Finally he saw the ship, called it
directly, and Dr. Rhodes' voice answered:

"What's the matter? What's up?"

Even as he was thrusting himself over the rocky
landscape, Bruce gasped out his discovery. He heard
his father's startled exclamation and then his father
called to Garcia for the charts.

As Bruce reached the ship, got through the airlock, and peeled off his suit, Garcia and his father had checked their charts with the oncoming asteroid.

"You're right!" yelled Garcia. "These charts have been tampered with! We've got to take off now. No time to lose!"

Dr. Rhodes pressed the warning buzzer. Arpad came dashing out of the hammock where he had been sleeping, and jumped to secure the various loose objects. Garcia assisted him, while Dr. Rhodes quickly determined their course and speed.

"Where's Jennings?" Arpad shouted, passing the control room for a moment.

"Why? Isn't he here?" Dr. Rhodes looked up.

"Oh, blazes!" he said. "He just left to do some outside observing! Call him, Bruce."

Bruce leaped to the radio sender, switched it to connect with the helmet phones of any space suit in outside operation and called. He knew that if Jennings was on the other side of the little world, he wouldn't hear the call. But within a second, Jennings' voice answered.

He hadn't gone far. In a few more minutes, he was inside the ship, divesting himself of his suit. Dr. Rhodes by this time was in a fury of excitement. Garcia had shown that they had bare minutes to take off.

In a mad dash for the controls, Jennings seated himself, Dr. Rhodes set the engines, and Bruce just had time to grab a hand strap before the ship tore off out of the surface of Apollo, and headed full tilt for the shining white disk that Bruce had spotted.

They made the asteroid on time. They settled down
again for another long wait, this time of a couple of
weeks, while their second asteroid sailed on its eternal
orbit through the bulk of the asteroids between Mars
and Jupiter. Their next stop would be Hidalgo.

But then Dr. Rhodes kept the charts in his possession
and after every observation made by anyone outside,
this finding was checked independently by someone
else and noted on a master chart that could not be
tampered with.

On this asteroid it was necessary again to make the
same type of study made on Apollo, for it had its own
peculiarities of motion, its own time of rotation.

As the members of the crew discussed it among
themselves, at first they felt that the mistake on their
original charts was an accident. But more and more
the conviction grew that it was deliberate. Someone
among their tiny group was trying to delay or even
prevent their trip to Saturn. There was plainly a spy
among them.

But they kept their suspicions to themselves as long
as they could. Meanwhile the work went on of chart-
ing the skies anew, of determining their location, until
finally one day one of the now many disks in the sky
was definitely identified as the little planetoid Hidalgo.

When it was finally in plain sight, Bruce stared at
it in fascination. No different apparently than its
thousands of brother asteroids, it alone dared out
farther than the rest. It had been to Saturn's orbit, it
would go again, and they would go with it.

Then finally the moment came, and the ship blasted

off once more. They crossed the thousands of miles of space between the myriad asteroids that now filled the view, and Hidalgo loomed larger and larger in their sky like a new moon.

They caught up with it, matched its speed and direction, and leveled down lower and lower, until at last their ship rested on its surface.

As Bruce prepared to make the first exit to Hidalgo's surface, a sudden thrill ran through him. The next time he made such an exit on a world, it would be out beyond where any man had ever been, out at Saturn's doorstep.

Chapter 7 Interplanetary Cannon

HIDALGO was only about forty miles in diameter, but it was nearly spherical, a little globe moving along in space on its own. Much too small to have an atmosphere, it was like most of its brother asteroids mainly rock, with here and there some glistening white patches which were frozen water or gases frozen into perpetual icy solidity.

In the days to come—for aboard the ship they still continued to measure time by Earth's twenty-four hours—Bruce learned to know the little world pretty well. They had a long stretch before them, and little enough to do after the initial period of star-charting which Dr. Rhodes had taken over entirely for himself. Bruce spent much of his time, aside from routine duties aboard the ship, in exploring the surface of Hidalgo and studying the changing wonders of the sky around them.

Aboard ship a certain uneasiness seemed to be everywhere. With so few in the crew and the knowledge that one of the five was a spy with the failure of the expedition at heart, no one felt like getting too friendly with others. Bruce and Dr. Rhodes could trust each other, but the old engineer was usually much too busy with his calculations to offer Bruce any companionship. Doubtless each man in the crew wondered who the Terraluna agent could be. Bruce thought about it a good deal in his wanderings.

He liked Arpad and found it hard to consider him a traitor. Yet, after all, who knew what another man might feel about things? Arpad Benz, who was of Hungarian birth, was a poor boy in his youth. He had not had many of the advantages that Bruce had enjoyed. He was a good friend, though given to a certain amusement at the actions of others. At first he had been rather patronizing toward Bruce, who wasn't really very much younger. But he had dropped that attitude as he had learned that Bruce was capable of hard work and good comradeship. Yet, would not the remembered unhappiness of poverty make Arpad open to tempting offers from Terraluna? Bruce turned that over in his mind. Was it not always possible that if a nice big amount of money were offered, money that would assure Arpad a good easy life the rest of his days, that it might make the young spacehand willing to betray the trip?

In his heart Bruce could not bring himself to believe that, yet someone aboard ship was a spy.

Garcia, the navigator, was a married man with two

children whose pictures he had stuck on the wall over his calculating machines. He was a kindly sort of man, a bit quiet, a man who had been on many trips and who seemed to be passionately interested in the success of this one, which would be his greatest exploit. Bruce couldn't figure Garcia as the spy.

Jennings was a brilliant pilot with a wonderful record. He had pioneered a number of space flights in the past, including the first trips to two of Jupiter's big moons. He was still young, in his late twenties, tall and serious. Bruce knew that this trip would crown his youthful career, make him in line for important posts in the UN space service, probably raise him in standing to the most valuable space pilot in the field. Surely, Bruce thought, he could not and would not sacrifice such a future.

And that left only his father and himself, two suspects who were out of the question. Could the tampered chart on Apollo just have been some error, some strange accident? Unfortunately, that seemed to have been ruled out.

He and Arpad went on journeys clear around the little world. Their weight was almost nothing, just as on Apollo, and after a little while they acquired great skill at propelling themselves in huge leaps that would carry them floating along in jumps of many hundreds of yards. They mapped out the surface for the exercise of it.

Though tiny, Hidalgo had many features that their imaginations could work with. There were miniature ranges of mountains—actually ridges thrown up from meteor scars or shrinkage as the little planetoid cooled over the course of creation. There were several really huge mountains, like great spikes sticking out of the surface, masses of iron that had projected from the surface as other parts had cooled faster. In a number of spots there was evidence of smaller asteroids or large meteors having buried themselves in the ground, leaving various hummocks or depressions. Around the other side of the little world there was one such meteor crater about three or four miles deep and wide enough at the bottom to house a spaceport all its own.

Speculatively, Bruce and Arpad amused themselves by imagining that this deep pit could serve as a space-pirate hide-out, just like in the stories they had often read. Actually, there were no space pirates—the problems of space flight were much too difficult for such things—but the idea was a thrill.

The sky above them was a constant source of amazement. They were passing through the bulk of the asteroid belt now and there were always dozens of them in sight. They took every shape and most of them were visibly in motion at differing speeds. Some between Hidalgo and the sun looked like moons of various phases. Others close by loomed large enough to show surface markings. Juno passed fairly closely; this was a big body whose surface was striped almost like one of the big outer planets. Not infrequently a puff of dust on the still surface would indicate the falling of a meteor.

As the days passed they came clear to the orbit of

Jupiter and the bulk of the asteroidal disks disappeared
from the sky. Then a new group came into view.

Garcia, who had gone out with the two spacehands,
pointed to a cluster of disks nearly overhead. "See
those? They are something really special. They're
what we call the Trojan Asteroids, the Fore-Trojans
to be specific, since there is another set of them. They
fly around the sun exactly in Jupiter's orbit, at the
same speed as Jupiter, but always the same distance
ahead of Jupiter. They remain in a cluster fixed
forever by the laws of gravity and mathematics."

"Why are they called Trojans?" asked Arpad.

"When they were first discovered, astronomers decided to call them all after the heroes of the war
between Troy and Athens in very ancient times. So
their names are Achilles, Ajax, Agamemnon, Hector,
Nestor, and Odysseus. The Aft-Trojans are also named
after these ancient heroes."

"Any good?" said Arpad, being practical. "I should
think maybe they'd make good space stations if we
ever develop travel to Saturn as a regular thing."

Garcia chuckled into his space phones. "I imagine
you're right. They'll probably do that in the next
hundred years after our trip is a success." He paused
and added:

"As a matter of fact, I believe there is an astronomical station there now, on Achilles. That would be
the biggest one near us. It'll be passing us by a few
hundred miles any minute now. See, you can see the
lights and shades of its surface now."

They gazed up. It was quite a sight, looming larger for a short time than the moon did in Earth's sky. They saw patches of brightness and dark spaces. The thought struck Bruce that if indeed there was still an astronomical station up there then it was the nearest they would be getting to other human beings for a long, long time. This lonely Fore-Trojan group would be their farewell point to other human beings. And another memory struck him suddenly.

"Say," he murmured, "I seem to remember reading about an asteroid mining base being set up on one of those planets, near the observatory . . . and if I remember right, it was a Terraluna expedition!"

"Awk!" exclaimed Arpad, while Garcia sucked in his breath. Then the navigator let out a sigh and said, "Perhaps, but I can't see that that need bother us any. Probably they know nothing about us. Still, I better tell Dr. Rhodes, anyway."

He swung off and glided back to the space ship. Bruce and Arpad stood watching the six bodies in the sky above them.

Arpad nudged Bruce. "A meteor," he remarked and pointed. A few hundred feet from the space ship there was a small cloud of dust falling back to the surface. Bruce looked. Even as he watched, another such spurt of dust went up in the air about the same distance on the other side of the space ship.

"That's strange," he remarked to Arpad. "Two in succession."

"Three," said Arpad, pointing to a third spurt rising near where the first one had struck.

Suddenly a cold chill ran through Bruce as it struck him what they were watching. "Those aren't meteors!" he shouted. "They're explosions! They're shells from a cannon! We're being shot at from Achilles! From the Terraluna base there!"

They started running wildly back to the ship, calling Dr. Rhodes on their helmet phone. Even as they ran, another shell struck, this time near where they had been standing.

Bruce shouted the alarm as they neared the ship. Dr. Rhodes called to them to hurry. They reached the ship, threw themselves through the airlock and slammed the door. Already Dr. Rhodes was buzzing the engines and Garcia was trying to activate the tubes. As the boys came through the lock without bothering to remove their space outfits, Jennings came from his sleeping quarters in a rush to the controls.

Bruce opened his helmet as he ran to the control room. Once there, he found his father at the controls with the ship already off the ground. "Father," Bruce yelled, "I know where we can take the ship. They'll never be able to hit us."

As his father shot the ship over the surface, Bruce told him of the deep meteor crater on the other hemisphere. If they put the ship down there, they'd be safe until Achilles was out of range.

Dr. Rhodes was personally flying the ship to that spot. Bruce had found their map of the surface and if they got to their hiding place in time, no cannon could reach them.

It was really easy to operate a cannon from an

asteroid. If you could line your sights, any simple artillery gun from even hundreds of years before could get enough power to break away from the weak asteroid grip and cross space to strike a visible target. Obviously the Terraluna mining camp had rigged up a cannon, knowing that Hidalgo would pass right in their sight, had awaited their chance, and bombarded the ship which they could see plainly through their telescopes. In a short while longer they'd have corrected their aim sufficiently to hit the ship and put it out of action forever.

As Garcia and Bruce were discussing this angle, their ship was already crossing over into the side of the asteroid away from the Fore-Trojan view. Bruce noticed that Jennings was standing by the radio, apparently fiddling nervously with the microphone. He watched Jennings' fingers tapping on the mike, and suddenly he realized that the radio sender was on, the lights lit on the dials. For an instant he was stunned.

"Stop!" Bruce yelled and made a dash for the radio. He tried to grab the switch but Jennings made a swing for him. Bruce twisted in his grasp, slammed the power control off the radio.

Garcia had started up in amazement. But Jennings grappled with Bruce. Then Arpad came up the corridor holding a wrench and joined the fight. Bruce was outweighed, but when Arpad raised the tool, Jennings suddenly quit, let go of the boy and stepped back, his hands raised. "O.K., O.K., cut it out. I'm through."

By this time Garcia had secured a pistol from their stores and held it on Jennings. "So you were the spy?"

Jennings nodded. "I'm the man. You ought to listen to me. You know this trip can't succeed. The odds are too high. If I could have stopped you, I'd probably have saved your lives."

"What if we'd been hit by those shells?" said Arpad.

Jennings shrugged. "Even so. We'd probably just lose our air, and have to abandon ship. The Terraluna base on Achilles would have picked us up safely. They have some small ships."

Dr. Rhodes glanced around from the controls. "Keep him under guard until we get this ship safely landed. We'll decide what to do with him then."

The ship crossed the asteroid, dropped into the deep meteor crater Bruce had discovered, and in the dark shadow of its bottom, miles beneath the surface, came to a rest.

They held a discussion. From where they were, the Terraluna guns could never reach them. Jennings admitted that he had not had time to let the enemy cannoneers know, by tapping in code on the side of the live microphone, where they were going.

But time was precious. In a little while, the asteroid mining ships from Achilles would be on Hidalgo itself searching for them. In time they'd be found.

Dr. Rhodes and Garcia conferred over their charts and records. They looked up. Rhodes glanced at Arpad and Bruce, then said, "We've got a very serious decision to make. We will have to abandon Hidalgo and go on by our own power to Saturn. We figure that since we have already acquired Hidalgo's own speed and orbital direction by riding on it, we only need to speed up and move ahead on Hidalgo's own orbit. We have the fuel, though it will leave us very dangerously limited after we reach Saturn. Our only hope of return, if we do this, will be to catch Hidalgo when it arrives near Saturn—at the very point where we had originally intended to leave it. If we delay on Saturn too long, we will miss that call and never return to Earth. I will ask you two to decide. The odds are long. Shall we do it? Shall we go on to Saturn days ahead of Hidalgo by our own power?"

Arpad was silent. Bruce hesitated. He wanted to say yes, but he felt that as Dr. Rhodes' son, that would have been expected of him. He'd rather Arpad made the decision. He turned, looked at Arpad. The other's eyes caught his. They had a merry twinkle, then Arpad's face broke into a smile.

"What are we waiting for?" Arpad said. "Let's get going!"

Chapter 8 Mimas

THEY abandoned Jennings on Hidalgo. This was not as deadly as it seemed. They unloaded and set up on the level plain outside their meteor crater hideout an airtight transparent tent, the type used by asteroid miners for short stays. They installed a small atomic-fueled heater and a spare oxygen purifier from their space-suit stores. Enough food for a couple of days was also placed in the tent.

Just before they left Hidalgo, they radioed the whereabouts of Jennings to the Terraluna station on Achilles, told them to pick him up. As soon as their call had been received and they knew that it had been noted, they signed off.

Bruce spoke with Jennings just before they abandoned him, as the task of setting up his tent had been given to him. The pilot was gloomy, but insisted he was right.

"Really, Bruce, in spite of your faith in your father's ideas, they are wrong. I tell you that Terraluna's research staff has proven positively that there would be no danger in their new mining project. I saw the figures myself—that's what convinced me that this trip to Saturn is very foolhardy, and that you're taking unnecessary dangers with good men for nothing."

Bruce shrugged, went on with his work. Finally he said, "If you felt that way, you had no right to come with us. If it's our lives that are to be lost, let us take that chance. Even if Terraluna is right—and I don't believe it—our own discoveries on Saturn's rings would be the final proof. If we're wrong, we'll find it out and say so. But no one, not even a powerful outfit, has any right to take a chance with all humanity while there's the slightest possibility of my dad being right."

Jennings looked at him. "I'll be sorry to see a smart young fellow like yourself get killed so early in life. Even if your father is right, he can't prove it by this trip. This ship isn't big enough to make the trip and get back. You haven't the fuel, and nobody can survive in the rings anyway. I'd have gone along with you if I felt that you had even a fair chance of success. But I don't. I'm an expert space pioneer—you know my record—believe me, I am sincere."

Bruce gritted his teeth but said no more. He felt that Jennings was giving his true views, and he had to respect the pilot's record. Yet he wouldn't let himself dwell on the possibility of failure. He refused to discuss any more. Besides, they had no time.

When they blasted off, Bruce caught a final glimpse

of the little bubble of transparent plastic that imprisoned Jennings. He wondered whether he would
be rescued in time.

They were edging just beyond the orbit of Jupiter at the moment of leaving Hidalgo. They blasted
along at full tilt for several hours, gaining tremendous
acceleration. Garcia had adjusted their direction so
that they were taking full advantage of Hidalgo's
momentum, yet directing their ship at a point where
Saturn would be long before the tiny asteroid would
arrive.

As before, they tried to conserve fuel. They would
turn off the engines and coast along for many hours
at a time. Had they been keeping the same distance
from the sun, they need never have turned their
jets on again—they could maintain the same speed
for millions of years since there was nothing in empty
space to slow them down. But moving as they were,
away from the sun, their speed was still insufficient
to break away from the great parent star's gravity.
When they coasted without power, the sun's grip
fastened on them imperceptibly, and in the course of
hours a slow dragging loss of speed was always de-
tectable. When the ship came back to a certain speed,
the jets had to be blasted on again and the lost speed
regained.

In answer to a question of Arpad's as to what would
happen if they did not use their jets again, Dr. Rhodes
said, from his position at the pilot's seat: "We would
continue to move outward from the sun along our
present orbit until we came to a dead stop some dis-

tance inside Saturn's orbit. We would then instantly start falling back toward the sun, following the other half of our same orbit until we fell faster and faster back toward the sun, perhaps as far as Mars' orbit. At that point we would swing around the sun and hurtle outward again, and we'd simply continue to circle the sun for a million years or so, just like any asteroid, until eventually we would fall into the sun itself and be disintegrated."

Bruce overheard that question. It helped make clear why the problem of their store of fuel was so important. He knew they had enough fuel to make Saturn and a little to spare. But any excess or emergency, and they would be lost.

The trip was long, long and for the most part dull. After the constant changing sights of the asteroid belt, there was little new to see in this vast space between Jupiter and Saturn, a distance of about four hundred million miles. Behind them, in crescent form, they could see Jupiter, a huge glow, visibly striped, with several of its great moons plainly visible as disks. Mars was out of sight behind the sun. The Earth could be seen just at the sun's rim, between them and that glowing body, which meant that only the night side of his home world was toward the Rhodes ship. To them the Earth was a faint circle of light, a ring around darkness, the ring being the reflection of the sun's glow through the atmosphere. Venus was invisible, lost in the sun's glare.

On the other hand, Saturn was slowly growing day by day.

It was at first a tiny ball of yellow with a thin, sharp line of white cleaving it at both sides. This line was the rings seen head-on. As they neared it and changed position, this line widened out, until it assumed the familiar form of the rings, circling the glowing golden ball like a wide halo.

As they neared Saturn, Bruce could see that it was belted like Jupiter. It had no surface markings, such as continents and water areas; instead, it was banded along its equator and upward with several wide areas of different colors. Some were near-white, others yellowish, or approaching orange or even bluish tinges.

All around the ship was the blackness of empty space, the stars of the galaxy glowing in the distance. Once, just once, a glowing sphere passed their view—a comet, Dr. Rhodes explained, that had not developed a tail and wouldn't until it came much closer to the sun.

Bruce spent most of the time in study, his father having insisted that he master the elements of star navigation and continue his mathematical studies that were so necessary to space flight. Garcia and Dr. Rhodes took turns, in their off moments, in drilling him in the various problems. They were hard and complex, but, as Garcia put it, "No harder and no more complex than the universe itself. If you want to play among the stars, you must learn the rules they play by."

In the passage of time, they approached Saturn. Its moon system was visible and quite impressive, even if you overlooked the ever-amazing rings. They held a brief conference as to where to establish their base.

Garcia was in favor of landing on Titan, the largest moon. "It's got an atmosphere of sorts, it's the biggest of the moons, almost half again bigger than Luna, and we'll be able to stand and walk fairly comfortably. We can probably find frozen water and oxygen around and build up our stores."

Dr. Rhodes, however, insisted on making their base the innermost moon, called Mimas. "It's only about a hundred thousand miles from Saturn, almost on top of the rings. It's tiny, about three hundred and seventy miles in diameter. This means that it won't take much fuel to go to the rings from there, whereas it will take a lot of fuel to get off Titan. Since Mimas has no atmosphere, our observations will not be clouded and will be absolutely clear. In every way, we should make for Mimas. It may be less comfortable, but it will be best for us."

So it was decided. Saturn had ten moons in all, three of them impressively large. But Mimas was the one they had selected.

By this time Saturn loomed large in their viewplates. Bruce watched as they narrowed in, under jet drive, for the landing. They passed Titan close enough to see that it had a soft glow around it, proving the presence of an atmosphere. Bruce knew from the astronomical records that this atmosphere was nothing that he could breathe. Any oxygen would probably be in frozen form, the air that it was com-

posed of would be thin, mainly ammonia and swamp
gas. But he could see that Titan had mountain ranges
and glistening blue-white areas that would have been
oceans and lakes if they had melted.

Mimas was a small crescent against the great glowing surface of Saturn as they closed in. Bruce had
the strange feeling that they were falling to the surface, that they would brush against the rings, so close
to these the little moon was floating.

Now, however, they came up to the outer side of
Mimas, and it filled their view, a black circle covering more and more of the sky. They swung around
it, circling down, and the ship was bathed in the
soft golden glow of Saturn. Down over rocky plains
and sharp jagged mountains until finally with great
skill Dr. Rhodes set the ship down on its runners on
a flat plain. They skidded over loose rocks, bumped
wildly, and Bruce could hear the thud of loose stones
against the metal hull. Finally they were stopped,
and the engines brought to rest.

For a moment nobody had anything to say. There
was a feeling of relief at the completion of the hard-
est part of their journey, a feeling of suspense at the
ordeals to come. Bruce never forgot that moment.
His father was still seated at the pilot's chair, leaning forward on his elbows, staring through the center
port, tired, his gray hair shining in the soft glow
from outside. Garcia sat next to him, his hand still
resting on the power controls, leaning back in his
seat as if about to fall asleep, his eyes relaxed and

closed. Arpad was just visible down the corridor at
the feed dials outside the storage tanks, slumped
down, one hand holding to a leather grip. Bruce
stood in a posture of tension near the airlock, face
close to the side port.

Then Dr. Rhodes straightened up, shoved away
from his seat, turned around and said, "Congratula-
tions, men. This is a new record for mankind. If
nothing else, there's always that."

Garcia jumped up, grabbed Dr. Rhodes' hand. "Let
us congratulate you, sir. It's your work and your
glory."

Rhodes smiled briefly, then his face sobered. "Perhaps we're all a bit premature. The time for slapping
each other on the back is not yet. The worst part
of the job is coming."

Arpad came up the corridor to Bruce. "What are
we waiting for? Let's get out and get our feet wet."

Rhodes and Garcia crowded around. "Let's all go
out together this time. We'll all pioneer a new planet."

All four got into space suits, attached helmets, set
their headphones. Bruce twirled the braces on the
airlock, they all crowded into the tiny closet-like
chamber, and the air pumped out. Then they opened
the front port, and, throwing down the short nylon
ladder, they climbed down onto the surface of Mimas,
Saturn's nearest moon.

They grouped around outside the ship. Bruce
looked about.

The ship and men were in a small plain, rather
flat but with many loose rocks lying about, those

which Bruce remembered the ship had struck in landing. He noticed that their landing runners were rather chipped and scarred, even bent in one place.

A series of low but sharp and bare red mountains bordered one edge of the plain. At the other edge an extremely close horizon gave the effect of a falling off into space only a quarter of a mile or so away.

The men were light, weighing not more than a couple of pounds each, which gave them heady feelings and made all of them lighthearted.

There was no air. The sky above them was black and they could see, Bruce remembered later, two or three large moons shining in the black part of the sky.

But that was afterward. For the moment all they had eyes for was the immense and fantastic vision that filled two-thirds of the great sky bowl above them. That was Saturn.

Chapter 9 Into the Rings!

LOOMING over the horizon, stretching far into the sky, over their heads, and glowing down greater than a second sun—though milder and muted, was the giant bulk of the planet Saturn. All four stood silent, staring at the magnificent vision, a sight more awesome than any they had ever seen.

Saturn was larger than Earth, something like ten times larger, and Mimas was closer to Saturn than Luna is to Earth. From its surface, at the point where they stood, it was like hanging over the Earth a few thousand miles up, when most of the sky would be filled with the view from below.

Indeed, for a moment, all the men had a curious feeling, that of looking downward, rather than looking up. The pull of Mimas was light, very light, and the bulk of the great ball above them so vast that it was like looking down from some ever-hanging cloud.

Arpad broke the silence, "Gosh, it's spinning! You can see it spin."

This was true, though not as dramatic as it might have seemed. But the surface of the great ball was indeed in visible motion. The surface of Saturn did not have continents and oceans and mountains like that of Earth or Luna or Mars. Instead, it gave the impression of a mass of clouds, of stuff lacking in solidity, missing in substance. There were bands of these clouds over the surface from end to end, from wide equator to the visibly flattened pole. Some bands were lighter, some darker; they varied from an almost white, a glowing cloudy white, to light yellows, and pulsing oranges and even here and there streaks of red and green and blue. In one part was a round white blotch. And because the great belts were irregular, had odd markings and colorings, it could be seen that they were moving. The planet was visibly rotating, and the more you looked, the faster it would seem.

Bruce said, "It is spinning, fast, too. Much faster than Earth looked from space."

Dr. Rhodes answered, "That's right. Its day is slightly more than ten hours long, and when you consider it is so much larger than good old Terra, its surface has to move terribly faster than what we are accustomed to."

"But is that the surface?" asked Arpad. "It looks more like clouds to me. Where is the surface?"

Bruce kicked a pebble without taking his eyes off the sight in the heavens. "I'll bet it hasn't got one. The spaceman's handbook says it's very thin stuff, and a very light planet for its size."

Dr. Rhodes answered, "That's right. The stuff of which Saturn is composed is even lighter than water. It very probably has no solid surface anywhere. There may be many meteors or chunks of iron and stuff floating about in its center, but I doubt if there is anything like a true crust anywhere beneath that cloudy surface."

"Ha," said Arpad, "why, you mean it's all mush clear through!"

Garcia spoke for the first time. "You know, I believe he's right, Doc. That's the word for it—mush!"

There was silence, and then suddenly something struck Bruce oddly. "Why, Father, where are the rings? They've vanished!"

Sure enough, the famous rings were not present. But then Garcia raised a hand, pointed out a thin white line that cut the planet in half and extended outward on both sides. "There are your rings. We're seeing them edge on."

"Yes," interjected Dr. Rhodes, "and that brings us back to the subject of this trip. Those are the rings edge on, and that's why I picked this particular spot. Because, do you know exactly how close we are to the outer edge of the outermost ring?"

No one answered, and he went on, "We are now only about thirty-one thousand miles from them. A short trip which we can make in one of our space boats—if we ever get the time to unload them and stop rubbernecking."

Bruce and Arpad took the hint. Reluctantly they took their eyes from the view above them, gazed at each other a bit foolishly, and then turned back to the ship. Garcia and the doctor followed them.

There was work to be done and they fell to. Because of the extreme lightness of everything, it was possible for them to move things that would have required cranes and crews of workmen back home. Bruce and Arpad themselves unlatched the rear hold plates, and carried outside the two space boats stored there, setting them up on the cleared plain.

The space boats were small rocket ships, hardly big enough to carry two men crowded into the small cockpit and a little cargo. They were designed as possible lifeboats, and also as exploration vessels. They were streamlined, bullet-nosed, all-glassine fronted, and they rested on large light wheels so that their noses pointed skyward. Bruce and Arpad fueled them from the ship's own tanks.

While they were doing this, Garcia and Dr. Rhodes set up a space tent, like the one they had left Jennings in on Hidalgo. To this tent they transferred their observation equipment, directional radio speaker, and other explorational devices.

Dr. Rhodes called the four together after a couple of hours had seen their tasks accomplished. "I'm not going to waste any more time. We can't afford it. So I am going to take off now in one of our boats to cross to the rings themselves."

He paused, but no one said anything. Bruce felt a pounding in his chest. Now that they were here, he realized what his father was daring.

"I shall take the boat across the space between, adjust myself to the outermost ring and work my way in among them. I plan to ride along, attaching myself to one of the larger particles that make it up, and there make my observations. I shall be as quick as possible and I shall return as soon as I have confirmed my discoveries. I'll keep in touch with you all the time by radio beam."

"You can't stay out too long," said Garcia. "These boats can't carry much food and water and their air purification system won't last more than two or three days."

"I understand that. But I don't expect to have to take too long. I want it understood that if I . . . if I fail to return or lose contact for over forty-eight hours, you are not to wait for me. You are to return home. These are my orders."

There was silence again. Bruce's heart pounded harder, but he said nothing.

Dr. Rhodes nodded at him and Arpad. "You two load my equipment aboard one of the boats. I'll take along two days' supply of sandwiches and fresh water."

They did this, while Rhodes and Garcia conferred. Then, finally, all was loaded. Dr. Rhodes, still wearing his space suit, got into the little rocket boat, waved a hand to them, slid the glassine covering shut, sealed it, and turned to the controls before him. The other three stepped out of range of the rear jets.

There was a brief moment, then puffs of smoke from the jets, and the tiny boat soared off on a tail of fire, shot into the sky, and rapidly disappeared in the direction of the glowing golden sphere and the thin white line of its rings.

They stared until it vanished. Then Garcia snapped, "O.K., boys, let's get to it. I'll take the first shift at the radio tent. You two get busy. Arpad, fix something to eat for the rest of us. Bruce, close up that rear hatchway, and stow away the spare junk and containers."

After his chore was done and he and Arpad had eaten—even though he felt too excited to want to eat—they both joined Garcia at the radio.

In spite of the distance, Dr. Rhodes was making good progress. He had gained a high speed very rapidly and now told them that he was simply letting Saturn's greater gravity do the rest of the work. His little boat was heading for the rings at free fall. He expected to be there in a couple more hours.

His voice came over the beam fairly well, quite clearly in fact, since their beam was directional and there was no atmospheric interference.

It was possible for a while to follow his tiny ship in their telescope—a contraption of reflecting mirrors set up on an open frame; an advantage that an airless world has over an atmospheric one is the wonderful ease of telescopic construction and vision. But so small was the ship that it showed only as a tiny glistening speck. As it neared the rim of the rings, it was soon lost. For seen through the scope, the rings were glistening and shimmering like the scales of a bright fish or like a flickering neon sign.

They worked and kept coming back to the radio. Dr. Rhodes was now rising above the outermost ring, he said, to effect a landing in the middle from above. His voice was tired, but elated. Bruce remembered that he had taken pills with him to keep himself awake for two days—and he took over the microphone from Garcia to remind his father to take one of the pills. Dr. Rhodes instantly responded, thanked him for reminding him.

Had he forgotten to do so in the excitement of his voyage, he might suddenly fall asleep from exhaustion —and risk total destruction.

In the tent, Garcia was hunched over the radio mike. Arpad sat on the floor, his head in his hands, listening. Bruce was slumped against the record table, taking notes on what was said. The floor was that of the satellite Mimas, flat, stony, pebbly. The sides of the glassine tent came down to them, stuck airtight by the nature of their plastic gummed edges, an invention in improved molecular self-adhesion that was one of the wonders of atomic plastics.

Now the old engineer's voice could be heard telling them that he was angling down among the tiny moonlets and meteors which composed the outer ring. He described what he saw and they could picture him drawing down closer and closer to the moving mass.

Now they began to notice static on the beam. A constant humming in the background, now and then a sharp squeal. Garcia kept touching the radio controls to try to clear them, but the noise was not on their end. He told the doctor about it, and Rhodes reported that their voices, too, were reaching him with interference and noise.

They could hear him talking about his near contact now. But the closer he got to his destination, the more the static howled. Now his voice was wavering, sometimes soft, sometimes loud, and they could not always make out what he was saying.

There were squeals and groans and growling sounds coming from their receiver. They heard Dr. Rhodes clearly for a moment, saying he could no longer make out what Garcia was telling him. Another louder series of screeches and ticking sounds came from the set. The noises grew louder and louder, until the little tent was roaring with the sound of eerie screams and ear-splitting hammerings.

By this time, they all knew that Dr. Rhodes must have begun to enter the ring itself. But the static was thunderous and they couldn't hear themselves talk. Then, suddenly, the tent was silent.

For a moment they were stunned. Garcia bent over the radio. He listened. There was nothing. "Not even a hum, not even his sending beam," he muttered to himself.

Arpad looked up. "Maybe he cut off his radio. If he got the same noises we did, he'd probably cut it off."

Garcia nodded slowly. "Yes, yes. I suppose that's the answer. I guess so."

"It has to be the answer," Bruce said sharply. "Has to be."

They looked at him, but said nothing. Suddenly he felt a cold horror reach into his heart. "It has to be the answer," he said to himself. He tried hard to shut out the horrible alternative.

Overhead the glowing ball of Saturn sped on, turning steadily, and shedding its soft cold light over their little tent. From the radio, there was only silence.

Chapter 10 The Stolen Space Boat

W<small>E'LL</small> keep a regular watch at the radio here," said Garcia. "If he comes on again, someone will be on hand at all times. We'll take it in shifts, three hours each."

The two younger men nodded. Somehow, now that they had lost contact, they felt helpless. Garcia was accepted in command, but they knew without asking that nobody would make any decisions not approved by the other two.

"Come, come," said Garcia, forcing a smile. "Let's not get down in the mouth about this. We had to expect some setbacks. I rather suppose it was nothing, just radio trouble. Probably the Doc will come back safe and sound in a half-day more and laugh at us for our worries."

"Oh sure," said Arpad, idly picking among the pebbles and sandy stuff that littered the bare rock floor. He picked up a rock, hefted it, tossed it aside. He idly reached for others, examining them. They seemed to be average pebbles, stony, some with traces of iron or rust.

Bruce noted his records of the radio conversations, noted the time, marked the time for the next watch. He put down his pencil and watched Arpad.

The young spacehand had picked up another small rock, was turning it over idly. "Someone lose a knife handle?" said Arpad idly.

Garcia shook his head, not paying much attention. Bruce narrowed his eyes. "What's that? Let's see it?" He reached down and took the object from Arpad's hand.

It was a knife handle, rather small, very worn, but a little odd. "Where'd you find this?" Bruce said excitedly. Garcia swung around then, startled.

"Why, right here, in the dirt on the floor," said Arpad.

"This is nothing we lost," said Bruce in mounting excitement. "This is something that was here all along!"

Garcia jumped up, looked at the object. Now Arpad took the fever, gathered around to look also. "Say, this *is* a strange object. It's certainly nothing that we ever brought along," Garcia said.

It wasn't a very remarkable thing, just a plain handle, made of some grayish material like a hard plastic, but clearly artificially constructed, with a couple of drilled holes in the end designed to hold a blade. When they examined it closer, they noticed a couple of odd geometric markings that seemed to be lightly impressed in one side of the object.

"This thing was made by some sort of intelligent life—something or someone here on Mimas before us!" Garcia said, expressing the thoughts that held them all.

"But," was Bruce's addition, "that means that once Mimas was inhabited!"

"Or else visited from somewhere else in the universe!" answered Garcia.

"Why don't we look around, maybe we'll find more!" Bruce said.

Garcia nodded. "You two go outside and scout around this area. See if you can pick up anything more. This is really important!"

Arpad and Bruce hurried out of the tent. Together they walked slowly around the plain in which their space ship stood. They would pause every so often, get down on hands and knees and sift through the loose rocks and sandy spots. For a while they found nothing more, until Bruce had worked his way to the area in which their ship had first come down, where their runners had carved a path.

He saw now that some of the larger rocks were strangely angular. Pushing some around, he noticed more. Calling Arpad, they explored the area thoroughly. There were many such angular rocks, and now in several spots they noticed that one or two such were still perched on top of others. Bruce found a little piece of reddish stuff, plastic of some sort, probably part of a machine, though he couldn't place it.

Arpad turned up some bits of broken material which looked like splinters of a smashed vase or pot.

When they came back to Garcia, and sat around and discussed their findings, they knew they had come across one of the most amazing discoveries in interplanetary history. Clearly there had once been a city standing in this plain on Mimas. A city that had crumbled into ruin and dust probably hundreds of thousands of years ago—and a city that defied all the logic of life.

Garcia explained this, "How could life survive here? There could never have been enough air here, even when this satellite was new and still hot from its creation. My guess is that this city was a colony planted from somewhere else. But where and who could it have been that was here so many lost ages ago—back before there were even men on Earth, in the era when the dinosaur and the lizard were the highest forms of life back home?"

For a moment their discoveries had erased their thoughts of the missing engineer. But now it was Bruce's turn to take over the radio watch, and instantly their worries returned. The radio had been silent for three hours now.

For the next twenty-four measured hours, one of them kept the watch, while the other two continued the exploration of the mysterious ruins. They no longer forgot their problem. As each hour passed, deeper and deeper dread filled Bruce's heart. Arpad was silent, lost in thought, and Garcia would make efforts at being cheery, but nobody responded.

The mapping of the city continued. There was very little substantial material left. The ages that had passed, even in the eternal quiet and preservation of airlessness, had reduced everything to near dust. They found a few more objects, bits of junk, pieces of broken jars, the sort of odd junk one might find on the fringes of an old trash heap. Everything they found was made of the same sort of plastic substance. In one or two cases there were fragments of rust that blew away at the touch. It was Garcia's theory that by accident this one plastic substance the ancient inhabitants had used was the nearest to permanence. It alone had survived the passage of the millions of years.

Of the nature of the builders, there was no hint. The knife handle, though smaller than a man would build, might have fitted a midget's palm, but that was the only clue.

Finally, after they had finished a meal together in the ship, and gone back to the tent in their space suits for a turn at the radio, they sat around in discussion.

The radio was still dead. Garcia looked at the two young hands, his face very grim. "We've got to decide what to do now. Our time is running out, we've but a few dozen more hours before we will have to leave— or else we will never leave during our lifetimes. Dr. Rhodes may still be alive; he has food and air for another day, a little more if he is careful. But we can't afford to wait. We must decide now."

Bruce said quietly, "We have the other space boat. I think we should use it to go after my father's boat.

Maybe we can see him. Maybe we can get in touch
with him from closer to the rings."

Arpad said, "That's a wide risk. It would be like
finding a needle in a haystack. It would leave us minus
still another man—and without any reserve space boat
if something should happen."

Garcia nodded. "It's out of the question. We dare
not risk it. If Dr. Rhodes couldn't make the trip, then
I don't think any of us are capable of making it."

Bruce argued again. But Garcia, after listening,
shook his head. "We have to act like good soldiers,
Bruce. Your father gave specific orders when he left.
We were not to wait more than two days. Our time is
almost up. We were then to leave without him. Our
obligation to him is to obey his instructions. Our discoveries here on Mimas will be his memorial. When
we tell Earth about them, they will send other
expeditions to examine them."

"Meanwhile," Bruce pleaded, "Terraluna will go
ahead with its Luna deep-core mining and my father's
warning will be ignored. We are risking all humanity
now."

Garcia turned to Arpad. "It's up to you then, to cast
the deciding vote." Bruce looked at Arpad.

The young spacehand looked away, got up, his back
to them, and stared through the transparent wall of the
tent to great Saturn in the sky. Finally he spoke without facing them, "Garcia is right. We can't risk it."

Bruce realized that his friend had had a hard decision. He choked down a last effort at protest. Garcia
put a hand on his shoulder. "Brace up. We've got

another day to wait. Your father may return before then."

Bruce and the navigator returned to the ship, Bruce to put things in order for a take-off, Garcia to calculate their course. Bruce went about his duties mechanically, his mind preoccupied with an idea of his own.

What was his true duty? he wondered. His father's life notwithstanding, the fact was that the life of all Earth was at stake if the Rhodes' calculations were correct. That, he felt, was more important than any one individual's life. If necessary, only two men could take their ship back to Earth. If he could go himself to the rings, could manage to radio back some proof of his father's theories, then nothing else would matter.

He was due for his turn at the radio tent next. Then would be the time. So thinking, he went about certain tasks of his own.

Arpad came back from the tent, took off his space suit, announced his intention to take a short nap. Bruce left for the tent to take over the radio watch, carrying a bundle with him. Fortunately nobody noticed.

Pausing at the tent for a moment to confirm that there was no response, he slipped outside and around the other side out of view of the ship. Then he made his way quickly to where the second space boat stood on its wheels, nose pointed at the sky.

Hastily, Bruce deposited the bundle of sandwiches and the metal bottle of oxygen he had brought with him. He knew he had filled the little rocket's tank when it was first set up. He checked its controls, then switched on its radio, and found it operating.

Then, drawing a breath, he eased himself into the control seat, closed the glassine panel and made the little rocket boat airtight.

From his cramped position in the nose of the little craft, he could see the glowing golden surface of Saturn, and almost in his direction, the white line of the rings' edge. He switched on the ignition, opened the throttle, watched the gauges indicate that his atomic fuel was flowing into the combustion tubes of the jets. He set his automatic governor, and glancing around once again at the still rocky plain and the low jagged mountains of Mimas, set his teeth, and pulled down the take-off lever.

There was a jolt that threw Bruce back against the cushions of the seat. He felt pressure against his body, and saw the mountainous edge of the plain suddenly draw near. He grasped the controls, pulled back, and the little rocket boat soared over the mountains, soared directly upward into the golden, glistening, spinning glare of Saturn.

He glanced for a split second behind him. The ship was already a miniature on a table-top moonscape. He fancied he saw a figure jump from the door, a tiny ant-like figure, but then he turned his eyes back to the unknown rendezvous he had made with a lost father and a cosmic secret.

Chapter 11 Look Before You Leap!

BRUCE buckled down to the job of getting to the rings. It was a thirty-one-thousand-mile leap, not at all simple even by the standards of his day. In an atmosphere the job would have been impossible in his limited time. But in the void of interplanetary space, where there was no air to slow down and to create frictional heat, the problem came down to one of speed.

The theoretical speed of the tiny space boat was without any limit. As long as its rockets blasted, just so long it would increase its speed. If it could carry as much fuel as a giant space ship, it could go as fast. Therefore, in practice the question was one of determining how much fuel could be used for how long.

The little boat carried a full load. The atomic fuel was hundreds of times more powerful than any of the chemical fuels of the dawn of rocketry back in the twentieth century. So this problem did not bother Bruce too much. He had power to spare for the work he planned to do.

If he coasted at a thousand miles an hour, he would cross the space in thirty-one hours. At two thousand, in half that time. But half that time would still be too long. At five thousand an hour, it would be roughly six hours. That also left little time for him. So he applied his jets as fast as his wide-open throttle would permit.

Bruce watched the dials before him on his small control panel. It was amazing how rapidly the speed grew. He felt the constant weight of his body as the tiny craft thrust forward at the top of a wide beam of blasting disintegrating material—a beam that left a swath of red and yellow behind him that stretched for half a mile before fading to invisibility. It took perhaps twenty minutes before the tiny rocket had reached the speed of twelve thousand miles an hour. He increased it still a bit more, then turned his engines off. The ship did not slow down, but, as happens in empty space, simply continued at that speed.

As Bruce watched, he noticed that his speed was slowly increasing, very faintly. This, he recognized, was the pull of Saturn, for he was plunging directly toward it. In the proper time, he would adjust his speed. He had about three hours to make his destination, the outer rings of Saturn.

He looked around him now, taking stock of his little boat. The rocket space boat was actually about the size of a small motorboat on Earth. The vessel was all enclosed, and the only living space was the cramped seat at the very nose, where the controls were. Just behind Bruce, underneath the leather-cushioned back of this driver's seat, was a small space for storage, in which he had put his food. Some purification was supplied by the air system, though this would not operate with the perfection of the big ships. On those craft, the air was completely purified and reoxygenated. In this small boat, which was never intended for other than short trips, it would keep the air breathable for two or three days, although it would become quite stuffy early. After that, the air would rapidly get worse, and fill with poisonous gases and fumes.

A Geiger counter and other devices for detection and analysis of space substances was part of the built-in machinery and registered on dials on the control board. Behind the air-purification valves were the engine, the tanks, the tubes, the mixing chambers, the electric system, and so on. This machinery, in fact, took up most of the tiny craft's space.

There was no room for space suits. The driver was meant to be wearing one—and Bruce was. He remembered this now, and checking the air system of the boat, unscrewed the front plate of his helmet so that he breathed the ship's air.

Before Bruce, the great mass of Saturn was now occupying the entire sky. He gazed down at its fuming, whirling surface, watching in fascination the changes going on. He could see how the edges of the various colored gas belts mixed with each other, clashed, and formed little whirlpools and storms, as each continent-wide belt moved around the planet at a different speed. There was a feeling of great turmoil, of excitement and unrest. And, above all, of something that instilled fear at the thought of plunging into it.

He seemed to be falling directly into this mass, into what would seem a boiling kettle of poisonous colors. Yet he knew that the temperature of these outer gas belts was probably far lower than anything he could bear. Perhaps, near the center of this monster planet, warmth existed. But before anything the size of his ship would ever get that far, it would be burned to a cinder by the friction of the fall.

A wide black band across one-half of the planet reminded him of the rings. That would be the shadow they were casting. And he focused again on the white line that marked their rim, edgewise to him.

It was already markedly wider. It was glistening and gleaming and sparkling, and slowly widening out. He knew it would be all too soon when he would reach that mysterious feature, that wonder of the whole solar system.

He mentally estimated where he would make his entry into the rings. He knew that the outermost rings revolved once around Saturn every one hundred and thirty-seven hours. His father had known this and had entered the ring at a point when it was first coming into sight around the edge of the planet. In calculating the speed of the ring and the time that had passed, Bruce figured he had to make his entry at a point where his father would now be if he had stayed at the original entry spot.

This was now about a third of the way beyond his father's point, but very nearly in line with Bruce's present direction. He directed his craft as close as he could to that spot in the ring. He adjusted his gyroscopic controls and blasted a bit to rise up above the rings as his father had done.

Now he relaxed and waited. He switched on his beam radio, adjusted it back to Mimas. Almost instantly he heard Garcia's voice:

"Mimas calling Bruce Rhodes. Mimas calling Bruce Rhodes. Will you call us? Will you call us?"

He hesitated a minute, then switched on his own answering radio beam: "Hello, Garcia. This is Bruce. Everything is O.K. I am on my way to the same point where Father disappeared."

Garcia replied instantly. "Come back, Bruce! Don't throw your life away! We have too little time. Come back while you can."

Bruce replied quietly that he would not. "If I don't return in time, go home without me. Don't try to persuade me. But let me know. Have you heard anything from my father?"

Garcia didn't argue. "Not a word. We haven't been able to locate him. Keep in touch with us at all times."

"O.K.," said the boy, "I'll not sign off."

They kept up a running conversation from then on. Bruce described the course he was taking, described the appearance of space from where he was.

He began to approach the rings. The edge of the other belt was now visibly wide and he could see that the sparkling was apparently caused by the fact that it was not solid as it appeared from distance, but that it was composed of innumerable little flickering dots. All these dots seemed to be racing along in unison, some turning as they went and evidently many irregular in shape. It was these irregularities that reflected the sunlight as they turned and produced the sparkling effect.

He elevated his ship and began to turn it to move alongside the belt at a speed close to that of the moving mass. As he rose above it, it widened out more and more until it seemed to him that a vast glowing yellow field stretched out for hundreds of miles of space, almost a plateau, a plain of seeming smoothness.

Then suddenly he noticed a small round dot apparently between him and the ring. Rapidly it came closer, then suddenly seemed to loom before him, a huge mass of white-lit stone plunging toward him. He touched the control of his boat, and it shot forward and the strange mass passed rapidly and silently behind him and vanished.

Bruce was alarmed. What was that? A meteor? A part of the ring? He talked it over with Garcia.

Garcia explained that it must have been a lone particle of a ring, one of the billions of such particles that made up the whirling halo around Saturn, but one that had not yet lost enough speed to travel in the mass. It was erratic, faster than most, therefore traveling along just outside the rings by itself.

"There must be thousands and thousands of such outlying bits and chunks of rock. The closer you get, the more you will find. You'll have to keep a careful lookout from now on. You may be able to estimate the speed of the ring-particles, but these are wilder."

Bruce was keyed up, on edge. He saw another approach, whirl past and vanish. Then more loomed up, a group of them, passing beneath him. Now he was beginning to near the edge of the outer ring.

And he noticed something on his radio. He had been so intent on the new danger that he had failed to realize that Garcia's voice was becoming obscured by humming, and that screams and squeals of static were beginning to come into the background of his reception.

"Garcia," he asked, "can you hear me perfectly? Are you getting static now?"

The noises were increasing greatly. When Garcia answered, he could hear part and then had to strain for the rest. But he knew the answer. Bruce's voice was being drowned out by the same mysterious static that had blanked out his father's voice.

Bruce would have liked to examine his radio apparatus, but it was built in under his control panel. Besides, the task of keeping on the jump to avoid the stray boulders and meteors that were now coming heavier and heavier left little time for that.

Now he was over the outer edge, several hundred

miles over at last and suddenly the sky was clear of flying dots.

Apparently these loose bits hung in the same plane as the rings. Whatever the original cause, the momentum and direction forced them all into the same level. Their speeds might differ, but rise above or below the level of the rest of the ring material they could not.

Yet the static continued. Now Bruce had time to examine his dials again. He saw now that one, which had been unmoving before was now wigwagging back and forth steadily. He looked at it and realized that it was the Geiger counter, the detector of radio-activity.

There was radioactive substance nearby somewhere. And he realized at the same time that this was the cause of the static, of the interference with his radio.

He explained this to Garcia, repeating and shouting, so that the squealing and screeching which his shipmate reported on the increase would not drown out his voice. Already his own ears were numb from the noise when he tried to hear Garcia. Finally, he realized that he had to do what his father had done. He yelled that he was turning the radio off, that they could no longer communicate because of the static. When he managed to hear a few snatches of Garcia's voice acknowledging, he switched off.

The silence was stunning at first. He had become used to the fact that for the last couple of hours his tiny space boat had been vibrating with voices and humming. Now all was silent save for the faint hissing of his air system and a clicking in his controls. The click was the Geiger counter, checking off the stray hits of radioactive particles.

Bruce realized that one small part of his father's theory about the rings of Saturn was correct. They were radioactive. Now the question was, were they so much so that to go into their midst would be to court death?

He thought about this a split moment, then shrugged his shoulders. He had gone this far. There could be no turning back. Death from radioactivity did not come at once. It would take days, weeks, months. He would have time to make all the observations necessary and to report them to Earth. Besides, the ship was insulated a bit and so was the suit.

He turned his ship and prepared to level down for a plunge into the coldly flickering flat plain that was the outermost ring.

Chapter 12 Marooned Among the Moonlets

A s BRUCE drew his little space boat down closer and closer to the glowing "top" of the outermost ring of Saturn, the seeming solidness gradually changed. What had appeared from far away to be almost a shining unbroken surface, became now a shifting mass, very much the same way that a diver leaping from a high board over a pool detects the tiny wavelets that move across the pool's surface as he plunges downward—wavelets that had not been noticed from his higher perch.

For a moment Bruce had the odd impression that he was diving into a golden sea. But this impression changed again as the sea seemed to draw apart into droplets, moving together in one great current, but still, droplets separate from each other.

He leveled his boat out to skim above the flow, adjusted his controls so that his speed caught up with that of the current, so that the glowing droplets now slowed down until from his viewpoint in the boat they were at last standing still.

This was an illusion, of course, because it merely meant that Bruce was now moving in the same direction they were and at the same speed. The effect was that of two trains rushing along parallel tracks together, so that the passengers could look out and converse with those on the next train—even while both trains were tearing over the ground. So it was with the various tiny shining bodies that made up the glowing stream of the rings.

Bruce, having reached what was now to be his basic speed, wherein the particles of the ring beneath him were now apparently standing still, dropped his little boat lower and lower, closer and closer. What had been droplets became shining dots, became now masses, separated more and more from each other by space. Bruce could detect the faint disk of one of Saturn's other moons shining through the ring, for the ring was by no means so tightly packed as to cut off all such stellar views. Stars could be seen through the mass as well.

The closer he got, the more the ring space opened up. And now almost before he realized it he was within the ring, moving with it, part of it. Before him there hung a great wall-like cluster of objects. Most were rather spherical in shape like tiny asteroids, many were irregular in shape, some were big, some small, and many were probably no larger than meteor nuggets.

Behind him a similar mass of objects filled the sky. On both sides and now above, other objects hung. Moving as he was at the same speed they all were, the effect was incredible for space—for the impression the mind got was that they were stationary, hanging in emptiness without support.

For a while Bruce simply sat and watched the eerie sight. Somehow, in all the trip he had simply never turned his imagination to what it would be like in the rings. Now that he was actually here, it all seemed so unlike what he had thought. He had somehow felt that the rings would be perilous, would be madly dashing in all directions, that it would be like being on a shooting gallery with lunatics firing machine guns in all directions. But this effect of stillness was something he was mentally unprepared for.

As he watched, he saw now that there were motions among the ring-particles. Some masses were slowly moving upward, others downward, and he noticed that a few here and there seemed to lag behind. He noticed now that two particles in front of him, one a great rocky sphere and another a small cubelike blackish chunk, were gradually drawing together. In a few seconds there was a slow bump, and just as gradually the two particles moved away from each other again.

The orderliness of the ring was not the result of any plan or system, it was simply the end product of millions of years of bumping and colliding, whereby the speeds of all the parts had been gradually slammed and shunted into unison, absorbed into each other, the faster particles gathering in one ring, the slower in another. The process was still going on, would undoubtedly go on as long as the rings lasted.

The sun shone through the ring and the light of Saturn shone as well and each little body was lit on one side and darkish on the other, just as if they were independent worldlets riding on their own instead of members of a vast crowd.

The Geiger counter was reacting wildly, and Bruce knew that the source of the radioactivity was here, in the rings. He suspected that the particles themselves were radioactive, but he knew it was his duty to check further. He picked a large mass among those in front of him, slowly increased the speed of his boat and moved toward it.

As he drew nearer, it grew larger and larger. With amazement it suddenly dawned on Bruce it was large, that it was perhaps a half-mile in diameter, bigger than many city blocks. Its size was not apparent from a distance. Bruce felt a slight chill as he realized that most of these ring-particles were big. If one brushed against his boat, it would not be the nudge of a pebble; it would be the nudge of an object whose momentum and weight would smash his little boat like an eggshell, no matter how apparently slight and slow the touch came.

The problem was one, however, that Bruce could handle. It resolved into the same thing as making a landing on a small asteroid. Bruce worked closer to the moonlet, down to its surface, which loomed up like a small world, and with scarcely a jar rolled his ship down in a groove on its side. He pressed his magnetic anchors out. The moonlet, like most cosmic material, had iron in its make-up. The little boat stuck fast.

Bruce closed the visor of his space-suit helmet, started his airflow, and opened the cockpit panel. With pick and drill fastened to his belt, magnetic shoes in operation, Bruce stepped out. Before letting go of his boat, he fastened a nylon rope to a stanchion on the boat's side and the other to his own suit. He dared take no chances. If something should nudge his moonlet somewhere, it might throw Bruce and his boat off.

Standing outside the boat, on the surface of a particle in Saturn's ring stream, Bruce looked about. Above him and on all sides, great rocks and tiny worldlets hung, apparently suspended in black space. Beneath his feet was a world, a very, very tiny one, whose horizon seemed to fall away fifty or sixty feet from where he stood. He seemed thus to be on a mountaintop whose sides would be very steep and precipitous.

The worldlet was mainly grayish, rocky, but where he had landed his ship was a deep sharp valley, dipping down a couple dozen yards. Having approached it from above, Bruce knew that this valley was a scar, a gash caused by some collision with another ring-particle, some time in the past.

He noticed that the scar had opened up the surface and shown up something of the inside of the worldlet. There were streaks of reddish ore, darker pockets, and in one space a curious outjutting, at the very lowest point of the scar of what seemed like shining metal.

Bruce worked his way along the scar, chipping off fragments of the various types of material, stuffing these fragments in the wide pockets of his space suit. These alone would be invaluable to the astronomers in their study of these rings.

As Bruce approached the shining outcropping, he became puzzled. It did not have the appearance of raw metal. Rather, it seemed like artificially worked stuff, like polished and hardened metal. He came up to it, stopped, mouth open in wonder.

His thoughts were right. The object was a part of a girder, the kind men use to build houses or bridges with. It was made of a hard and polished white metal, but it was part of a structure of some sort, beyond all question. He could see the holes where rivets might once have been, he could see that it was made of several pieces of worked metal, joined together in some type of welding. It jutted out from the scar, the bulk of it buried in the rock and mass. He could see now that there were scratches and linings revealed at the bottom of the scar showing other parts of building.

He stood staring, his mind a whirl of emotion. He tried to imagine what a building girder would be doing some dozens of feet underneath the surface of a rocky moonlet. He gazed at the scar for some time, remembered now various cracks and lines in the surface of this ring-chunk. A chill suddenly coursed its way down his spine.

Somewhere, at some time, a building had stood on an open plain, in sight of the sky. Or perhaps it was a bridge, or a railroad trestle. Something had happened to that plain, to the place where the building had stood. It had been torn apart, ripped out like a piece of hand grenade is torn off, and crushed like a piece of mud in a strong hand. The plain, the rock on which the building stood, had simply folded up on it, engulfed it, buried it, crushed it and covered it.

And it had taken the accidental collision with another such chunk to tear aside the hardened rocky fist and reveal the secret it held in its eternal grip.

Bruce's mind whirled at the thought. Suddenly he felt sick, sick with the discovery he had made. He sat down by the girder, put his head in his hands.

Gradually he felt better. But he still refused to try to put the clues together. He suspected the answer, but he wanted to put off bringing it into his conscious mind until the danger of his present position was abated.

He tried to break off a piece of the girder, but it wouldn't even scratch. That was not surprising, considering what it had apparently resisted so far. But bending down and searching along the very bottom of the deep cleft, he was able to come up with several handfuls of gravel and dust among which he spotted shiny particles that had probably been sheared off from the girder or other objects like it when the collision had occurred. These would do perfectly for analysis back on Earth, and he put these handfuls into his pocket.

He made his way back to his little space boat, deposited his samples in the storage box, unhooked his nylon rope, and got back into his control seat. Closing the panel, he took off carefully until he again floated in the midst of the current of ring-chunks.

He worked his craft slowly along, letting his speed lag so that the stream began to move slowly past him. He decided he would try and find another particle that might have further evidence of artificial construction. Many went past him, most of them seeming to be rocklike meteors, others spherical, but without anything in sight that looked promising.

Then he saw one coming along that was not spherical. It was a blackish mass, roughly cubical in shape and probably not more than a couple of hundred feet along any side. This held promising irregularities. He eased his way over to it, brought his little space boat against it, worked his way into a pocket in the blackish mass.

The magnetic anchor didn't seem to work. Bruce wasn't upset; in fact he was hoping to find something that would not be a typical meteor rock. This time when he opened the cockpit panel, he attached the nylon rope to his suit before getting out. Taking another such rope from the locker beneath the seat, he eased out and carefully roped the ship down, tying it bodily to the little moonlet.

He knew now he had a real find in this particular chunk. It was nonmetallic, it had the appearance of dirt frozen into great solidity. In one place, a white band proved in fact to be a streak of frozen gas. A small sample bottle in his pocket was good for that. He opened the bottle, and what air there was inside simply vanished into the near-vacuum of space. Then he chipped off bits of the frozen gas, forced the snowy chunks into the bottle, capped the bottle again. Back in the ship, when the bottle warmed up a little, that gas would melt. It would enable Earth's chemists to determine something else about the origin of these rings.

Impressed into the black substance were shapes that looked like vegetation. He knew that any particle in these rings had probably been pounded by all the others innumerable times over countless ages. Anything recognizable would long ago have been pounded flat. But flat or not, the stuff would yield to analysis. And Bruce felt sure that what he was standing on was a chunk of forest, or plant-bearing ground, a chunk that had been torn away, folded up and crushed in the same giant fist that had shattered the place of the broken girder.

Knowing that he was holding treasures that would add to the history of the universe and to man's understanding of existence, Bruce worked his way back to his space boat, loaded with samples. He bent over the open cockpit and started to stow his samples away.

Suddenly, without warning, there was a terrific jolt. Something seemed to strike him a thud on the back. He almost lost his balance. The ship rocked. When he regained, looked around, he saw to his horror that a small meteor-like moon-particle, not more than a foot across, had bounced into the end of his boat and bounded away into the void again.

It had shattered the engine. Bruce was stranded.

Chapter *13* Strange Static

STUNNED, Bruce stood and stared at the tiny round meteor the size of a basketball drifting back into the black disk-strewn sky. It was hard to believe that anything that seemed to be so light, as to bounce, was in fact hard iron or stone, whose weight was sufficient to crush the engine section of his rocket ship, shatter it as if it had been struck by a steam-driven hammer.

But there it was, the damage was done. He looked into the ship. The front half was intact, what had been struck were his tubes, his wires were wrecked, torn, his carefully tooled vents cracked, and his fuel was fizzing away in a cloud of vapor. The little boat would never be able to fly again. Bruce was now without any means to return to Mimas, to return to Earth with his invaluable information.

In the past few minutes he had come to realize that he held the answer to the problem his father had

posed, the question that had brought them all the way
out here against the opposition of Terraluna. He knew
the secret that Saturn's rings held—and now he could
never reveal his secret.

For it was an important one, the most important
probably that men had faced in their history, one that
might result in the greatest error that any intelligent
species could make—their own self-destruction.

Briefly, what Bruce had come to realize, to figure
out from all the bits of evidence that had been put
before him, was this story:

Once, millions and millions of years ago, when
Saturn was still a young planet and had not cooled
off as much as it had now, it radiated sufficient extra
heat from its own surface to add to that of the sun
and make its nearest satellites warm enough to sustain
life.

At that time, when life on Earth was limited to
scaly dinosaurs and crawling lizards walking about in
steaming fogbound tropical jungles, Saturn had no
rings. It had an innermost satellite, a large one, large
enough to hold an atmosphere. And on this moon
there had been life, and among those living things,
one creature had learned to use tools and to talk and
to pass information to its young. This creature developed a civilization in the course of time, used metals,
built cities, discovered machinery, and at last discovered the use of atomic energy.

They had reached out a bit, investigated their fellow
Saturnian moons, built colonies or cities on them—
such as the ruins on Mimas. They had explored and

dreamed of the conquest of the universe. Perhaps they may have sent space ships as far as the savage primitive Earth, and come back to report it a dangerous and terrible place to visit.

In the course of their work, they discovered the need to dig for the atomic elements that made their cities run and factories hum, the deep-hidden heavy metals that were so vital to atomic work. And they had discovered what astronomers and geologists of Earth know, that the heaviest elements sink to the core of a planet when it is created, and that it is in the heart of a world that they must dig to find what they need.

And so the ancient Saturn moon-men invented deep-core mining. And they invented the same processes that Terraluna was now preparing to use on Earth's moon.

They had gone ahead with their atomic blasting, had gone down into the very center of their satellite, and rocked it with the vibrations and shocks of atomic releases. The satellite was close to Saturn and its gravitational pull. It was under the stress of constant shifts in the gravity pull as it moved around its parent planet. And now the series of super-atomic blows at the center of the moon added to the strain and it was too much.

One horrible day that moon of Saturn must have been broken apart, blown up, and shattered into bits. Torn by Saturn's pull, struck at its heart, the fragile crust cracked and smashed and was blown apart.

Some part of the moon escaped into outer space to

wander forever as meteors or to fall flaming into the sun. Some fell into the soft mass of Saturn to burn briefly into ashes and gas. But a great part of the moon's wreckage continued to travel around its parent planet, following the course that it had followed when it was one single mass. Instead of one body, however, there were now millions and millions of tiny pieces.

Some of the pieces were moving faster than others, depending on what part of the satellite they had been when the blowup occurred, others moved slower. So some circled the planet and caught up with their slower brothers.

For thousands of years great confusion must have existed—constant collisions, constant flares as particles continued to fall into the parent planet. But in the course of the endless years, gradually the odd bits were sorted out, gradually a pattern was established. By the time the lizards of Earth had lost their leadership to certain soft-skinned, two-legged creatures, and these same bipeds had learned to control nature and to build telescopes, Saturn had its rings.

That was the secret of Saturn. That was the meaning of the ruins on Mimas, of the girder on the moonlet, of the crushed mass of forest land on which Bruce's wrecked rocket boat rested. That was the meaning of the radioactivity which seemed to be present in the rings—even after these millions of years, the atomic blast's mark was still felt.

There was no doubt in Bruce's mind that he had all the evidence he needed to convince Earth of the danger of deep-core atomic mining. He believed that even Terraluna would accept the facts without further argument. Nobody, certainly, could want to see Luna shattered, to see Earth bombarded with its parts for years to come, to see the Earth become a ringed world —and a ruined one.

But—how could he now bring this news back? Had he made his discovery too late? It would certainly be a cosmic joke on mankind if he failed now.

Bruce wandered about the little ring-particle, thinking. Time and again he wondered about repairing the ship, but it was impossible, completely impossible. If, he thought, he could at least radio his findings back to Arpad and Garcia, then they could carry the news. It would not be in vain.

He returned to the rocket boat, closed the cockpit panel. It still seemed airtight. He started the air pump to fill the little tiny cabin. It seemed to work, and then he noticed that it was a losing proposition. There were cracks. He couldn't quite succeed in building up any amount of pressure.

The controls were working, the radio was working. He switched it on. There was a roar of static, of radioactive interference. He moved the directional beam control. For an instant there was static silence. He suddenly became all attention.

Bruce shifted the beam slowly. Now he saw that the moonlet on which the ship rested was acting as a shield. It was not radioactive. He supposed that, because it was not iron or rock, it had long ago lost the charge from the initial explosion. When his beam was pointed at the "ground," the interference was blanketed.

Just what good this would do him, he could not at first determine. Yet he felt that somehow it was a first step to the problem at hand. He emerged from the cabin, looked around. There was a pit in the ground nearby, a hole punched by some meteor at some time in the past. He untied the nylon ropes that anchored the little rocket boat, and then dragged the craft over to the pit. It would fit in, and he pushed it so that it floated to the bottom.

Drifting down to join it, he again tied it down, got into the cockpit. Now the craft was in a hole, open only at the top, on all sides and below was the insulated shield of the coallike particle. He adjusted his beam to reach out directly above, and tried it.

Again there was a roar of static, but this time he was able to detect the various tones in it. He had blanketed out all but the one small sector above him. All the interference he would now get would come only as moon-particles passed by.

By carefully tuning his receiver, he was finally able to have some control over his reception. He would get momentary periods of near-silence, when for a brief instant no great mass would be passing overhead or in his way. There were instances when he knew he would be able to send a message or to hear one if by luck Mimas was in his direction when a message was coming.

The little moon-particle was spinning rather slowly,

so that in the course of time his little beam opening would cover most of the directions around him. Unfortunately his time was limited, by the amount of food and air left—and that was little. He could not tell whether Mimas would happen to come under the focus of his radio in that time, and whether also no static-producing moonlet would not be between him and it to ruin the hope of reception.

He stuck to his radio, listening, sending out calls. For several hours he hung wearily to his cockpit, in the blackness and darkness of the ring-particle, watching the slowly moving lights of the other particles slowly drift overhead, hearing the rise and fall of their passage in the humming and screaming of his radio, sending out his message every time the noise was low.

Then, as he felt himself almost dozing off, he thought he heard an irregular sound, a staccato *dot dot dot*. He leaned closer to his phones, listened. Amid the humming, amid occasional screeches, he again heard the faint faraway sound. It was code, of that he was suddenly sure, but he could not read it, it was too faint and too irregular.

He looked up, expecting to see Mimas' disk visible through the haze of the ring. But it was not there; instead, the glowing surface of Saturn was there and against it the dark line of the inner rings. The signal was not from Mimas! It was from the other direction! It must be, it had to be, from his father!

His father was alive then! A surge of energy ran through Bruce. Suddenly he felt that the cause **was** not lost. He strained to hear, but the sound was faint, and fading again as a moonlet swam between him and the inner ring.

He stuck with his radio in earnest, calculating the moments when the particle's motion would bring him again into line with the inner ring. After a half-hour of agonized waiting, he again heard the code. It was faintly stronger, but still not quite strong enough to make it out.

He wondered if he should try to send a message, then decided against it. If he could not understand his father's calls fully, he should not risk a message until the time was ripe. He carefully spotted the exact direction the code was coming from, left the rocket boat and got out of the hole.

He watched the inner ring from there. Somewhere in the next ring must be where his father was, and he presumed that Dr. Rhodes must have been disabled even as his own little ship was. Bruce understood that the rings of Saturn revolved at different speeds. The outermost one was the slowest. The next faster, and so on, until the nearest one whirled around the huge planet in only five hours.

Dr. Rhodes, then, was on the inner ring from his, and slowly overtaking Bruce's position. In a while he would pass the spot where Bruce's own particle was and go on, eventually passing around the planet and out of hearing . . . probably forever.

They were like two riders on a merry-go-round, the one on the faster turntable passing the other slowly but certainly; first narrowing the distance as the faster rider came up, then passing closely side by side, and finally traveling away from each other.

This was the position of Bruce and his father. At the moment, Bruce noted with a glad heart, his father was obviously overtaking his son's position. They would probably not pass each other for a dozen hours or so.

This meant that Bruce would get his father's signals so much clearer in the next hours that they could communicate, and perhaps, just perhaps, figure out some way out of their problem.

Bruce couldn't imagine what such a way would be but knew that while there was life there was hope. But he knew also that the wherewithal of life, for both of them, measured in terms of air and food, was running steadily lower and lower.

Chapter 14 Jumping Jack

ow followed a period of anxious waiting, Bruce crouched in the cockpit seat, listening at his radio as the scattered code appeared and disappeared, noting with the passing of time how it grew steadily louder. During an interval he managed to eat, closing the cockpit panel, stuffing the visible leakage points with paper and wadding until the air loss was reduced to a slow leak. In that time he was able to open his helmet, gulp down a couple sandwiches, a couple vitamin tablets, another antisleep pill, and as much water as he could drink.

The code was coming in stronger, though still badly distorted by static. Bruce opened his own key, directed his sending beam toward the inner ring:

"Calling Rhodes; Bruce calling Rhodes. Can you hear me?"

Intently he listened, but the code continued to come

on its wavering course. Again he opened his key, called. Still no evidence of response. He listened to the monotonous dot and dash, now fairly steadily audible. Again he sent out his call.

The dot and dash continued for a second or two, then suddenly stopped. A humming came on, and then, far away, he heard what seemed to be the tones of a voice. But amid the squeals and moans of the ring static, he simply couldn't make out what the voice was saying.

He gritted his teeth in his impatience, opened his key again: "Bruce calling Rhodes. I can hear you. Can you increase power? Bruce calling Rhodes."

Again he heard a voice replying, but still it was muffled, drowned out. He wondered if this was all to be a ghastly teasing, nothing. He tried again. Listened again. Now he seemed to make out a word or two: ". . . Rhodes . . . fuel dis . . . to . . ."

He called again, asked for a repeat, strained. Now he had luck; during a lull in the constant static barrage he distinctly heard the voice. It was that of his father:

"This is Dr. Rhodes. Stranded here by failure of fuel distributor. Can you come to me with replacement? Where are you?"

Bruce opened his key. "This is Bruce on outer ring. I am wrecked myself. Cannot come to you. Can you suggest advice?"

The reply came back. His father's voice, now faint but still clear. The engineer was excited, wanted to know how Bruce had got there, then told Bruce not to answer, to stick to fundamentals. "How badly is your boat wrecked? Is your boat's fuel distributor still intact? Can you remove it? Look quickly, we may be able to figure out something."

Fortunately, one of the things that Bruce had made himself familiar with during their long journey outward was the design of rocket jet engines. He knew where the fuel distributor should be. He got out of the cockpit onto the ring-particle's surface and walked around to the broken side of the boat.

He was able to unbolt the siding that covered the vital parts of the engine and remove it. He peered into the mass of wires and tubes and valves. The little boxlike device that played the part on an atomic rocket that a carburetor used to play on an ancient gasoline engine was there, unharmed. The bouncing meteor had passed it by a few inches, shattered all beside it, but the fuel distributor was good as new.

Bruce fumblingly detached tubes and unscrewed wires from the box, worked it out of the engine, shook it free of a few drops of atomic fuel. He carefully brought it forward, deposited it beside him in the cockpit.

Now he opened the radio again. It was a few minutes before he could again contact his father.

"I have the distributor here. It is O.K. What shall I do now?"

His father's voice came back. "Listen carefully. Take down my location. You must try and come to me, and bring the distributor. It is our only chance to get back. You must bring it to me. If I have this one part, we can both return in my craft. My own ship is otherwise all right, but the distributor was faulty, and broke completely. I have not been able to repair it."

Bruce announced his readiness to try anything. He could not imagine how it would be possible for him to go to his father without a ship, but he felt that one might as well try anything. "How are you fixed for food and air?" he asked.

"I've a little, but not much," came his father's reply. "You have no time to waste. Besides, judging from your radio position, I am catching up with your position on the outer ring. You must not let me pass you or you will never catch me. You must start now. Listen . . ."

He talked for several minutes, giving Bruce directions as to how to proceed. Bruce opened his radio for one last second: "O.K. I'm on my way. Keep talking so I can locate you."

He snapped his sender shut. His father's voice was now audible over his helmet phones, though no longer understandable in the uproar of static and electronic interference. But it was understood that his father's voice was to serve as a guiding beam for him to follow, much as an airplane follows a radio beam to its airport.

Bruce stuffed the spacious pockets of his space suit with as much food as he could stow. He carefully strapped the little boxlike fuel distributor to his belt. He pulled the seat out of the cockpit, unscrewed the three small oxygen tubes stowed there, strapped them to his back.

Now, with a wrench in hand, he climbed to the

back of the small boat, tore open the cowling and plates, exposing the entire innards. The long tubes of fuel stood exposed, the exhaust valves, the smashed parts, reams of wiring in many colors. He found the tube he was looking for, a yard-long plastic cylinder, fitting into the mixing chamber. This he carefully unscrewed, making sure to avoid any chance of the cylinder's contents escaping. He lifted this cylinder clumsily out of the boat, stood it on the ground, and easily leaped down to join it.

Taking part of the nylon ropes that held his boat to the ring-particle's surface, he turned the cylinder valve end down, and strapped it to himself, so that he straddled the thing like a witch on a broom, his feet hanging down.

Looking briefly around, looking at the small rocket boat which was now beginning slowly to drift and roll with the motion of the little moonlet, he gazed upward.

The great glowing mass of Saturn filled the sky, bathed everything in a golden glow. Against its surface he could see the thick black line of the next ring inward. Between himself and that line, a half-dozen moonlets hung, part of the outer ring like his own. He spotted the nearest one, a small body, several yards wide, perhaps a hundred feet away. He braced his legs, and suddenly jumped upward.

Weighing practically nothing, he shot up into the space between. Almost before he could catch his breath, the tiny round ball grew larger, and he barely had time to brace himself before he hit it.

He grabbed its surface instantly, held himself from bouncing off again. Beyond hung another chunk, this one rough and rocky, several times larger. Again he braced, jumped. He nearly missed it, but got a hand on it as he almost passed it, and pulled himself back.

From there, the darkish ring-particle where he had left his ship was already small, the boat a mere sparkle against its side. Again he jumped, this time a longish distance to a huge sphere, several hundred yards in diameter.

This one, though rocky, held promise of interesting discoveries. But he was not on an exploring trip. He was traveling, by jumps, from worldlet to worldlet. He drew breath and jumped again to a farther ball.

All this time his father's voice was coming through, in snips and snatches. For a moment he could hear a few words, then a new series of screams and howls would cut in from the radioactive moonlets.

When he could hear anything, it sounded as if his father were describing his trip and his theories of the moonlets. He gathered from scattered phrases here and there amid the interference reference to intelligent life and to ruins. Evidently his father had made the same discoveries that Bruce had made.

Now Bruce began to feel a little uneasy. The ring-moonlet where he had left his ship was out of sight, lost in the mass of shining disks behind him, they in in turn making a vast glowing belt across the black sky. He was alone, utterly alone, without a ship, without a means of feeding himself, with nothing but a thin space suit between him and death.

Above him more moonlets and yet more moonlets blocked the way. Again and again he jumped, and gradually as he did so the space cleared. He saw the black outer edge of the inner ring grow clearer and the space between him and Saturn grow less clustered with black balls of moonlets.

He became quite skilled at his jumping progression. He learned how to estimate the strength of his leg push, how to steer himself in the correct direction without having to fumble, he dared take longer and longer leaps, picking the larger bodies to aim for, thrusting himself upward, floating through emptiness, watching his target grow, twisting his legs under him, landing asprawl, the great tube tied to his body kept from touching the rock and thereby cracking.

At long last he saw that the edge of the outer ring was at hand. He made one final moonlet, and stood now, silently staring.

The tiny worldlet beneath his feet was shining softly in the Saturn light. Its horizon curved away a few feet from where he stood. Beneath him he could look down into a bottomless pit in which swam countless lights, beyond which he could see the vague face of one of Saturn's large moons. Looking out to his sides, he seemed to feel himself standing on a large flat plain, stretching shining and soft across the sky, the illusion of solidity caused by the unending parade of millions and millions of fragments, reduced by the processes of the ages to a certain unison of direction and speed.

Above him shone the huge round bulk of Saturn, a molten sea, its belts of swirling gas like veils concealing a mystery that none might ever look upon. And before him, seeming but a step away, was another ring, a flat circular platform to his eye, darker than his ring, but still glowing silent and untenanted in the sky. Between him and that other platform seemed but a short distance, a narrow gap over starry depths.

Bruce knew that this was a dangerous illusion. This was no narrow step, no close-lipped abyss. This was a space that was not a few hundred feet or even a few miles wide. It was a gap two thousand two hundred miles across! It was like the distance from New York to Denver, taking the familiar measurements of his homeland's geography as a guide to understanding.

Could a man cross such a space in one leap?

The answer, astonishingly enough, was yes. Bruce understood that. That was the trickery of outer space. If you weighed nothing, if you start yourself in motion, and there is nothing to slow you down, no air to push against, no force to pull you back, then you will continue to move with your initial speed forever. Forever, that is, until you do hit something, or until something pulls you to it.

That was not the problem. If Bruce leaped now, he would eventually fall into the next ring. But the question was: when? With all the strength he could muster, he would probably still take many, many days to fall across that gap—even though great Saturn would actually be drawing him also, speeding him slowly toward it. In that time, his air would foul, his suit's heat be lost beyond the power of his small belt battery to restore it, he would starve.

He had to cross the belt fast, at space-ship speeds. He had to speed up to be able to come alongside the particles of that ring, which were moving a good deal faster than the ones he stood on, whose speed was now his own. He had to aim himself to hit the one spot in that vast ring where his father waited, to hit it without delay, in a matter of hours, as few as possible.

His father had told him of a way. No man in all the history of space travel so far had ever needed to try it. But now Bruce poised himself. *Ready,* he said to himself. *Set,* his mind ordered, and then, *Go!*

He braced himself, grasped the long cylinder from his boat firmly, and hurled himself upward and outward into the gap between the rings, into the empty space that separated them. Astronomers back on Earth had named this gap. It was known to them as Cassini's Divide, after the ancient astronomer who had first detected it. And now Bruce was moving into this Divide alone, moving across it.

He was a lone figure, a strange one to try to cross such a distance. A bulky, airtight, electrically warmed coverall was his space suit, fitting him like a loose pair of jumpers. On his feet small metal soles provided magnetic attraction when needed. A pack on his back housed his tiny atomic-activated battery, which supplied the current for his suit, the power for his radio. Twin tubes forming part of the pack supplied his oxygen, fitting into a marvelous little purifier drawing in and revitalizing the air steadily. Despite this device, the power of the suit's air supply was strictly limited, in a day or so the amount of poisonous elements in his air would be more than could be removed, then suffocation would set in.

On his head a glassine, metallically reinforced helmet allowed him vision in all directions. A visor on the front could be opened if necessary when there was air pressure on the outside. A small but powerful portable atom-radio made up a flat pack attached to the suit's chest, and its phones were built into the helmet. The wide pockets of his suit were bulging with the fragments he had taken from the ring-moonlets. A container on his belt held the fuel distributor and a sack of sandwiches. A huge canteen swung from another part of his belt.

But it was the cylinder which now dominated the picture. Bruce was astraddle it, and the cylinder head was down. As he moved away from the ring edge, outward into the void, heading on toward the bulk of Saturn, Bruce manipulated the valves on this cylinder. As he turned one, he felt a vibration in his finger tips, and a sudden thrust to his body. He felt as if something were dragging him forward, felt the cylinder seem to struggle in his hands as if trying to escape.

The cylinder contained inert gas, under great pressure. This was used in the rocket jets to dampen the inner effects of the blast and to occupy the fuel tank space left empty by the exhaustion of fuel. The gas was not fuel itself, but it was necessary to the safe and practical application of the atomic explosive fluid used.

But a rocket operates on a very simple principle, and even a flow of gas from a cylinder or a balloon can move the object it is escaping from if the weight is low enough. As a small boy, Bruce had seen toy balloons whiz around a room when they sprang a leak and the gas whizzed out of the side. In effect, this cylinder, packed with tremendous quantities of gas under great pressure, was such a balloon, tremendously more powerful.

Bruce had no weight. The release of the gas from the cylinder, forced out through a tiny nozzle, created a genuine rocket effect, no different in any way from the principle used in the space ships. This cylinder's thrust held to Bruce's body, directed by Bruce, made the boy a miniature space ship in fact, if not in outward appearance.

He directed his motion toward the point in the ring from whence his father's voice came. Or rather toward a point ahead of it, knowing that by the time he reached that point, there his father's ring-particle would be. The constant thrust of the cylinder, as its gas drove through it, created a steady acceleration. A fast one, ever faster. If the gas held out, Bruce should be able to cross that Divide at a speed almost equal to that which his little rocket boat could have given him.

Onward he floated, the cylinder vibrating in his hands, the radio squealing, his father's voice becoming ever clearer in his ears. Before him the huge hemisphere of Saturn loomed; he seemed slowly falling toward it. Behind him the inner edge of the outer ring was rapidly drawing away, its surface flattening out, glistening. Above him he could see the face of one of Saturn's moons, mottled in white and gray, as the sunlight was reflected from its barren valleys and mountains. On all sides, beyond Saturn, there glowed the millions of brilliant pin points that were the stars beyond the solar system, the unimaginably distant suns.

It would be hours, Bruce knew, before he could reach his destination, in spite of his now terrific speed. He clutched the cylinder, stared ahead, listened to the sound of his father's voice amid the humming of his radio.

Dr. Rhodes had set himself a hard task by using his voice as a guide beam. He had to keep talking for hours, without knowing whether Bruce was hearing him, without being able to get a reply. At first, it had seemed to Bruce he was reading out of an astronomical manual, for Bruce caught snatches of talk about distances and measurements and galactic weights. Then, after a time, Bruce's father evidently exhausted this topic and began to talk about his trip. Bruce missed the opening of this in a long burst of static, but picked up the thread of his father's voice along about the time that he was coming down for his first entry into the rings. Bruce heard:

"I noticed that my reception was becoming worse and worse and wondering whether my ship's radio was going on the blink. There was constant static, and a steady loud humming. I found I could no longer make out what was being said to me from our base at Mimas. By this time, I was nearly into the ring, and the moonlets that made it up were already visible. As I came nearer, the static grew completely unbearable, and I reluctantly found myself compelled to shut off the radio entirely. I realized that this might cause some anxiety back at the ship, but it was quite useless to continue. I hoped that Garcia would realize that this static was because of the closeness of the rings, because I knew now that they were radioactive."

Bruce nodded. Somehow none of them had thought of that, all had apparently assumed there had been an accident. His father went on to tell of his first landings on the ring-particles, discoveries and experiences much like Bruce's. He had not had the good luck to spot evidence of artificial construction, though. Nonetheless Dr. Rhodes had seen enough to support his theory that the rings had been caused by an atomic explosion.

"I decided that the material on the inner rings might have been closer to the heart of the original exploding satellite, because of their greater speed. I therefore took my boat out of the first ring and went on to the second. I realize now that I should have tried to communicate with you on Mimas then, but I was far too excited about my discoveries to think about radio."

Dr. Rhodes went on to detail his entry into the second ring inward, his exploration of a couple of moonlets there. His voice went on:

"I now went on to a third moonlet directly at the edge of the ring. I had noticed its odd sheen, unusual since this ring's particles are otherwise considerably darker than those on the first ring. The moonlet was solid rock, but oddly polished along one side. Time and other particles had pounded it, yet it had not lost its curious appearance—it appeared to have been deliberately smoothed out.

"I brought my ship down, and clamped it tight. When I got out, I discovered that my imagination had not deceived me. The moonlet was as smooth as marble, far harder, and definitely the product of artificial work. You can imagine my extreme excitement. This moonlet was a chunk of some lost city, of some civilization that had grown and died suddenly, long before there were men on Earth! I went along the marble. It seemed to me to have once been a floor somewhere, perhaps on a city square, but probably on some hilltop, for the moonlet was shaped like a cone.

"Then, imagine my further surprise, when I saw that there was a metal disk set deep in the center of the marble flooring. It was below the level of the rest of the stone, and that I suppose was why it had survived the battering which it would have received over the ages. I got at that disk, and found that it still bore the signs of ornamentation, of some kind of carving. I tested it, then realized that it rang hollow and that it covered an air pocket beneath it!"

Bruce listened, fascinated. He was about halfway now, apparently hanging in emptiness, with the edges of the rings on either side appearing like the thin milled edges of coins. He went on listening to his father.

"After a couple hours of work I was able to bore a hole through the metal lid with my hand atom-torch. I worked slowly because I did not want to disturb anything underneath that lid. I was finally able to pry it open, for it turned out to be on hinges, whose grips had long ago turned into dust.

"Inside that marble fronted ring-particle was a tomb. It was a tomb that must have come out of the ancient past of that Saturnian moon race. I imagine it must have carried the same relation to their final civilization as, say, ancient Egypt does to our own. We men of science do not leave such grand tombs behind us any more. We build no pyramids for dead kings, and we do not store the treasures of our culture there for their imagined revival in some pagan after-world. Perhaps that is a mistake, from the viewpoint of future archaeology, because of what I was now seeing.

"There are treasures in this moonlet, treasures beyond conception. There is a carved stone box here, which must once have held the individual who had died there. That body has long since vanished into dust and air. I found nothing. The shape of these lost intelligent creatures is still a mystery. The box was of a curious size, it would never have fitted a human body. I cannot quite imagine what sort of an odd shape it would have fitted, for it bulged at the wrong places.

"I found tools and metal ornaments, tarnished, but preserved wherever they were made of metal. I found hints of dust where wood or cloth things may have been, bits of metal that may have been buttons. The walls are covered with inlaid gold inscriptions, in some alphabet I cannot begin to decipher. Unfortunately I can find no pictures, no symbols that made any sense to me. But I am sure that trained students of these things could piece together a remarkable story."

Bruce was slowly nearing the edge of the inner ring. He directed the flow of his cylinder's jet always in the direction from which his father's voice came the strongest.

"When I returned to my ship, I had a number of things to bring back. I loaded, and decided to rig an atomic buzzer here so that we could locate the particle again. When I tried to start my engine, I discovered the ship would not work. I tried again and again. Finally I opened up the rear, and found that somehow a tiny meteor, no larger than a pebble, had shot through the boat while I had been inside the tomb. It had put a hole through my fuel distributor, wrecked it, but left everything else intact.

"So I was waiting here, hoping that someone would come from Mimas. I am glad it was you, Bruce, although it was a dangerous thing to do. If you can reach me, soon I hope, we will be able to get away and return. I have enough fuel, but my air is low, and I have not eaten in ten hours."

Bruce gritted his teeth. He was nearing the edge of the inner ring. He saw that his speed was still not quite that of the moving particles, which he could now detect. He increased the flow, twisted his body so that the cylinder moved and now he was speeding up, moving alongside the ring.

In a short while he was running up close to the edge of the inner ring. He could see the moonlets, close-packed, one upon another rolling through the heavens in their unending tight parade. For the most part they did seem darker than those he had noticed before.

He listened as his father's voice grew louder, despite the increase of the humming and static as he was getting nearer to the moonlets. He moved along, faster than the particles, straining his eyes to find one which would be brighter than the rest. It was like trying to find a needle in a haystack, but fortunately this particular needle was calling out to him.

On and on he moved, his eyes wearying of the constant strain. Now and again he imagined he would see some brighter body among those visible at the edge, but each time as he neared it he realized that the radio voice was coming from beyond it.

He glanced down at his cylinder of gas, and suddenly realized that it was getting low, that the dial which registered its internal pressure was nearing the zero mark. He knew he had only a few more minutes left to him.

Now he thought he saw another little moonlet, different in texture from the others. He moved again toward it, angling inward. And then he noticed a tiny spot against its shining surface, the tiny bullet shape of a rocket boat. And as he rushed toward it, he saw a tiny man-figure standing next to it, waving his hand.

There was a strange change in Bruce's body pressure. He seemed suddenly held back. He looked down. The gas had stopped. The cylinder was empty.

Chapter 15 Skip the Hoop

RUCE was still moving. In space there was nothing to stop him; but he had calculated on the continued extra drive of the cylinder to bring him to the surface of the moonlet. Now that that power had died, he saw that he would drift past, miss the surface by several feet—but that would be enough. There was nothing for him to push on, no way he could see to bring him that extra distance or to alter his direction of free float.

He waved his hand wildly, pointed energetically at the cylinder, hoping that his father would understand his predicament. He heard his father's voice, "What's wrong? Can't you make it?"

Bruce waved more. He couldn't attempt to speak to his father yet, the interference would have drowned out his weak space-suit radiophone which was designed only for conversing over very short distances. He waved to the cylinder again.

His father's voice came on again. "Oh! The thing's empty! You can't get any more power. Well, now . . . listen to me. There's still one more thing you can use that cylinder for, and you'll have to do it right. First, unstrap it from yourself."

Bruce showed he understood by doing so, wriggling around clumsily and freeing himself from the long gas container. All this while he was drifting after the ring-particle, nearing it but at a wider and wider angle.

When he had untied it from his suit and was holding it to him by his hands, Dr. Rhodes spoke up, "Do this right and do it carefully. Grab the cylinder, swing it in the direction opposite that to which you want to go. At the proper moment, when you're closest to me, throw it away from you as hard as you can. This should have the effect of pushing you in the opposite direction, according to the laws of rocketry, based on an equal reaction for every action."

Bruce understood this. He followed instructions, swinging the yard-long plastic container around until his own body was directly between the moonlet and it. He continued his free drift, until he saw that he would get no closer to the surface. At that point, he shoved the cylinder away from him with all his might.

The empty container shot away fast. Bruce himself moved away from the point of the throw in the opposite direction, but much slower, for he was many times bulkier than the cylinder. But it was enough. In a few more minutes his feet brushed against the polished marble surface of the moonlet. His father caught him, drew him down, and they clung together in mutual relief and joy.

Dr. Rhodes looked tired and worn. Bruce could see his face through the glassine helmets they wore. But the old scientist's eyes were still sharp and a smile of determination was on his lips. They held each other and looked at each other in pleasure. To see another man in this lifeless cosmic wilderness was pleasure enough; for father and son to see each other was a moment of delight in kinship, a delight that was rare indeed. For each had worried about the other from the moment of leaving Mimas, though neither had permitted that worry to interfere with his duty toward humanity's safety.

Bruce pushed his father toward the space boat, and without the necessity of words, they both got in, closed and sealed the cockpit. Unloading the food he had brought with him, Bruce would not permit his father to attempt anything until he had first eaten.

Dr. Rhodes swallowed the last crumbs of a sandwich, and said, "We've got to move fast, Bruce. Our air is limited. No more time-wasting now. Let's get that engine fixed."

They closed their helmets, and climbed out of the rocket boat. Dr. Rhodes took the fuel distributor that his son had brought with him, and got to work replacing his defective one with it. Meanwhile, Bruce stowed away the samples he had taken with him in the space beneath the ship's seat and behind the seat.

"Why don't you go and take a look at that tomb, while I'm finishing this job?" said Dr. Rhodes over their helmet phones. "It may be the last chance for anyone to see that in many years—maybe ever."

"Why's that?" said Bruce, picking his way over the marble surface of the strange little moonlet toward the depression and the metal-gleaming door he could see.

"The chances of any future explorers finding it again are very slight. Even with an atomic buzzer, they may never be able to pick it out among the countless millions of other moonlets. So you take a look too."

Bruce made his way down through the opened metal covering and stood with his space-suit flashlight gazing around. It was as his father described, a tomb that had been old when the Earth was but a steaming jungle and cave men were still a thing of the far, far future. The emptiness of space, the cold of a sunless darkness, had preserved much, but the very disintegration of elements alone had served to destroy most of the tomb.

Bruce saw the weird coffin, realized as his father had, that no human form could have fitted it. And then his father called to him to hurry back, the ship was ready to go.

He made his way out of the tomb, then turned and carefully closed the round thick metal disk that sealed it. When he saw it was tight again, he paused, and in a moment of boyishness, drew a small tool from his belt and scratched his initials in a corner of it, along with the date. Then he straightened up and moved across to join his father.

He climbed into the cockpit, pulled the transparent cowling tight. They were cramped, elbow to elbow in the narrow space. Bruce thrust his helmet visor up as soon as the air-pressure gauge registered safety.

The air was already rather stale and he could smell oil and ozone. "Let's go," said Dr. Rhodes, and, switching on the activators, pushed the throttle. They were off!

They swept away from the ring-particle easily, swung around, away from the mass of the parading particles, moonlets, and fragments. Being on the edge, they simply turned tail to Saturn's glowing bulk and swung out into Cassini's Divide.

This time Dr. Rhodes turned the ship outward over the rings, piling on speed, drew them upward at a slant from it. "Locate Mimas, Bruce," he ordered, his attention on the problem of clearing the rings and any stray meteors that may have been on their way to crash into Saturn.

Bruce scanned the sky. One glowing disk he recognized as Titan by the fuzziness that surrounded its outline against the black sky—this was the atmosphere of that largest moon. For a moment Bruce wished they could visit that strange world, a place almost as large as a planet, whose air was poison, whose lakes and rivers were ammonia, whose polar caps were frozen oxygen, whose life, if any, would be beyond any conception of biology.

He spotted other moons in various positions on this side and beyond. Rhea following Titan closely. Enceladus emerging from eclipse on the other side. Tethys off to one side, a narrow crescent. Mimas was at an angle from them, downward from where they were, beneath the ring, whereas they were above it.

He directed his father. They swung further upward. "It's the wrong side we've come out on," his father said. "We'll have to jump the hoop to make it. I don't know if our fuel will hold out."

He increased their speed. They passed over the shining flat surface of the outer ring, a thousand miles high. Really quite close. For a period they seemed to be flying over what could almost be thought of as an ice field, strangely partly transparent, for they could see the brighter stars through it, so considerable were the spaces between the myriad fragments that made it so seemingly solid. The sun, a small but still terribly bright ball, shone upon it and sometimes caused dazzling reflections.

At last they crossed the width of the outer ring. Below them they could see the shining globe of Mimas, a white and gray mottled moon. The ship swung toward it, moved past the still thick-appearing edge of the ring, and headed for its home base.

Bruce switched on the radio. "Calling Mimas. Rhodes' boat calling Mimas. Garcia, Benz, answer, please."

He switched to reception. The rings now past, there was but a faint humming. Reception was clear, but he could hear nothing. Dr. Rhodes muttered under his breath.

"They should have been on watch."

Bruce said quietly, "Don't hold it against them. After all, I did desert them, you know. It's hard for only two men to keep the watch by themselves. It would be lonely, it would be something that would make each man gloomy and upset. Besides, by this time they may not be on watch all the time. Perhaps they have work to do."

He could see his father was impatient and tired. It was understandable why he should be easy to anger now. "I suppose so, my boy," he said. "I guess I shouldn't expect too much. It's just as hard to wait without word as it is to be active."

Bruce stole a glance at him. He knew what his father meant, for surely Dr. Rhodes had waited in near hopelessness himself. "We'll probably find them too busy playing chess to pay attention to our call," he joked.

They neared Mimas, the small moon growing larger and larger. Its mountains and plains became visible. Bruce kept up their radio calls, but still there was no reply. He was becoming very uneasy himself, but he said nothing about that.

Their air was becoming distinctly bad now. He felt a drowsiness stealing over him, remembered that he still had oxygen in his suit tanks, and reached a hand over his shoulder and switched that on. The faint hissing of his reserve supply came into the cabin. In a few moments their heads cleared.

His father said slowly, "That was a timely thing. I think we'd have been asleep by now if you hadn't thought of that. But I think we don't have much more reserve."

They were nearing Mimas now, coming down over the wide hemisphere of it, searching for the particular plain and mountains where their ship had landed. Finally Bruce thought he recognized the spot. "Over there, beyond that chain of saw-toothed mountains. I think that circular-shaped plain is the place where we landed."

The little rocket boat soared over the tops of the sharp-edged mountain chain, passed over the lower, gentler mountains that ringed the plain, and came down over the flat wide surface.

"Look!" shouted Bruce suddenly. "There's the ship —and it's moving!"

They saw it at the same time. The space ship was there, on the plain where they had left it. And the ship was moving slowly on its runners, a stream of fire pouring from its rear jets.

Bruce yelled into the radio, "Stop! Stop! Garcia, we're here. We're coming! Don't take off now! Don't leave without us!"

His father reached out, his face taut, and a hand flicked a little button marked *Emergency Signal*. Ahead of them, on the nose of the little speeding rocket boat, there was a puff of smoke, and a tiny rocket shot forward to explode in space a half-mile away beyond the moving space ship on the plain, and leave a shower of brilliant sparks and a cloud of blazing gas.

On the plain, the space ship continued to move forward, slowly gathering speed for the take-off, a stream of atomic rocket fire growing wider behind it as it accelerated.

When Bruce had taken off after his father in the second rocket boat, Arpad had been napping in his hammock aboard the ship and Garcia had been at the calculators in the control room working out the problem of their return.

The sound of Garcia's running feet in the corridor had aroused Arpad and in a few minutes he was outside too, gazing upward, although the tiny boat was long out of view.

They had gone to the radio tent then, and had tried to make contact with Bruce. Eventually they did, and they stuck with him until the moment when the ring static and the radioactive interference blanked out their reception and Bruce had switched off. For a while they stayed, then decided they could not afford to keep on watch, now that there were only the two of them.

They returned to the space ship, arranging with each other for one of them to step out every hour and check the radio for any messages.

"My calculations of our return course are not entirely complete," Garcia said, "and I've got to finish them without any more delay. Meanwhile, you had better check the fuel tanks and let me know exactly

where we stand. With both rocket boats gone, there's
a lighter load and this may cause new figures to be
set up."

"Well, surely you can wait a couple days at least
before we decide," Arpad argued.

"I hope so, but I will know definitely when I finish
these figures. Frankly, the outlook is not too good."
With this reply, Garcia went back to his charts and
his machines.

Arpad went on to the rear, clambered about the
tanks checking their capacity, tracing the wiring, put-
ting everything in shape for a return voyage. He felt
very ill at ease, dreading the moment they would have
to make a decision. Although he had often kidded
Bruce during the trip, he had come to like him a lot,
and he felt that Bruce's action in going off to the rings
was the kind of thing that he wished he could have
done.

As they ate a meal together, Garcia and Arpad discussed the decision facing them.

"I'm sure they're going to return," Arpad said.
"We've got to have patience."

"I'm afraid that's just what we can't afford to have,
Arpad," said Garcia slowly. "I completed my figures
just a few minutes ago."

He waited. Arpad put his fork down, stared a
moment at Garcia's sober face. "And?" he prompted.

"We've exactly three hours and twenty minutes
more, before we must take off. If they don't return in
that time, we've got to leave without them. Otherwise
our next chance will be in five weeks. We haven't the

fuel for the longer journey then, and the risk will be far greater, perhaps much too great."

The three hours having passed, Arpad stood outside one last time and looked for a sign of a rocket boat. Against the awesome display of Saturn in the sky, he still saw nothing. Stepping inside, he closed the outer door, went on, sealed the inner lock door. Taking the post Bruce had held by the side port viewer, he called to Garcia. "Ready!"

Seated at the forward controls, Garcia glanced over his dials. He moved a switch, then another. There was a subdued humming as the generators started up. He gave a nudge to one of the blaster buttons.

The ship jolted as a puff of atomic vapor burst from one rear tube. Another such and the ship swung around slightly, then more until it was facing the longer plain, Saturn to its rear.

Garcia looked at his clock. He was early by about three minutes, but he preferred to take no chances on split-second timings. He pushed several buttons.

Its atomic jets blasting, the ship moved slowly forward, began to gain speed. For an instant Garcia noticed a puff of smoke and a burst of stars in the sky in front of his ship. His mind, intent on his keys, dismissed it as a meteor explosion.

Arpad, hoping against hope, had stood with his face pressed against the viewer gazing after the rings, at the section of the sky where he had hoped to see the missing men appear. A split second before the burst of the emergency signal rocket, a buzz on the board in his engine room caused him to turn his head away.

It was only the warning that another tube was in motion. When Arpad looked again to the outside, the signal had vanished. Finally he turned away and bent to his task of watching the steady flow of the engine.

The ship moved ever faster. Garcia, tense, piled on speed, his eye on the clock. He had never driven a space ship of this size entirely under his own direction before, and he wanted to keep the risks down. The fear that he might make deadly mistakes haunted him and he took the ship off the ground, over the mountaintops and into the interplanetary void.

Chapter 16 Sentinel from Below

BRUCE and his father watched tensely. The space ship was moving across the plain and gathering speed. They were approaching it from the rear and, unless their emergency rocket had been seen, they would not be noticed. The ship lifted off the ground, started to rise steeply upward to clear the tops of mountain rims.

"Oh, no!" Bruce exclaimed. "No! Not after all this!"

But Garcia and Benz in the ship could not hear him. There are no moments in space travel as attention-consuming as the take-off and the landing. Right now, having failed to spot the little puff of the rocket signal's explosion, their attention was concentrated on the controls and the engines. As the two Rhodeses watched, the ship moved faster and faster, and within a matter of seconds vanished from view into the black airlessness of the sky.

Their little boat swooped down for a landing near the spot the ship had just vacated. Neither father nor son said a word as they skidded to a stop. Both felt a deep empty feeling, felt as acrobats would feel when suddenly the cushioning net is withdrawn.

For a little while they just sat there in their seats, exhausted, feeling let down, unwilling to organize their thoughts. Bruce finally twisted in the cramped seat, looked around. He nudged his father. "They've left the tent up," he said.

Dr. Rhodes looked to where Bruce's finger was pointing. "Hmm," he mused, "maybe they mean to return then?"

Bruce had a suspicion that they had been marooned permanently, but he could not allow himself to voice it. "Yes," he said, "we should have realized they would not abandon us. Maybe they are going to the rings themselves to try to locate us?"

The older man nodded. "Perhaps; we can only hope that some such thing is the case. Let's go and see if they have left any supplies for us in the tent."

Shutting their helmets tight again, they slid back the cockpit panel and hoisted themselves wearily out of the little space boat. As they moved toward the airtight plastic tent, Bruce felt the stiffness of his muscles, the body-tiring ache of the long hours without sleep, without proper exercise or good air. They reached the tent, unzipped the side opening, and entered.

Sure enough, there were several cases of condensed food, a cask of water and a portable purifier, and three long tubes of oxygen. The radio had been removed, though a few tools still remained.

"If they planned to return, why did they take the radio?" asked Bruce suddenly.

His father shrugged. "Let's not think about it now," he remarked. "Let's get some food and rest first. We are in no condition to tackle the problems ahead of us. When we've had some sleep, we can think this matter through."

Suiting their actions to their words, they allowed the air pressure in the tent to build up a bit, opened their helmets, and gulped down a meal. Next they spread themselves out as comfortably as they could on the hard rocky floor, and before they knew it they were both in deep sleep.

To Garcia's surprise the ship made speedier timing than his calculations had called for. They made their take-off from Mimas without any trouble—and also without ever noticing the tiny space boat that came down from the direction of the ever-glowing rings. Headed as they were away from Saturn, they had not thought to look back. Garcia was intent over his dials and over the controls that directed their ship. Benz in the engine room was concentrating on the readings, unwilling to allow his mind to rove elsewhere.

By the time they had cleared the weak gravity field of Mimas and were accelerating to break free of the great field of Saturn itself, it was apparent that the ship was making better time and gaining speed faster than Garcia had figured. He watched the readings with wrinkled brow, wondering whether he had not been too hasty, whether he should not have waited just a few hours longer.

He voiced his thoughts to Benz over the ship's communication system. Arpad answered, "Wouldn't your figures be off if the ship were lighter than you had estimated? Wouldn't we then move faster?"

Garcia was silent a moment. "Yes," he finally said, "you're right. But . . ."

Arpad broke in. "But you had been figuring on Bruce and the doctor being with us. Wouldn't that account for the error in your figures?"

"You've hit it," Garcia said. "Of course I had counted on a load of four men, not two, and also on having at least one of the space boats aboard ship. This way we are considerably lighter than planned, and therefore we are making the trip much more easily. Perhaps we ought to go back?"

"Can we?" asked Arpad excitedly. "If we can, we should!"

But then Garcia's voice came again, "No, no. It would be impossible to turn back now. Suppose we found them? Then my old calculations would again be right, and with the heavier load we'd have, plus the delay of hours in starting and the lesser fuel reserve due to this start, we could never make it. We shall have to carry on now, whether we like it or not."

There was silence on the ship as the two men pondered the unpleasant truth. They continued their acceleration, heading for Hidalgo somewhere in the black void beyond the Saturnian system.

Bruce woke up many hours later. For a moment, as he opened his eyes, he could not imagine where he was. Above him the thinly transparent plastic roof of the tent allowed some of the stars to shine through and the great glow in the heavens to cast its weird light on them. Bruce lay quietly for a moment, then turned over and got to his feet.

His father opened his eyes, looked at him. They smiled at each other. "Well, Bruce," the gray-haired engineer said getting to his feet, "dawn of a new day. What's for breakfast?"

Bruce laughed. "Powdered eggs, vitamin pills, and wheat concentrates, topped off with a nice cool glass of water, flavored slightly with chlorine and assorted chemicals. Tuck your napkin in and join me."

They managed to keep their spirits up as they ate. Then, unable any longer to keep their minds off the main problem, they stood. "What now, Robinson Crusoe, Senior?" asked Bruce jokingly.

"Ha!" his father said. "That old shipwreck had it easy. He may have been marooned on a desert island. We are marooned on a desert world." His face sobered up instantly. "Let's face it, Bruce. We have only a few days here at best. We've got to figure out what little we can do in that time to justify our trip. I don't see any way out."

"Well," Bruce said slowly, "surely there is something that we can do. If we have enough fuel in our little boat, maybe we can at least go to another moon and find frozen water and air there. Maybe we can make it to Titan. Even if the atmosphere is poisonous, perhaps we can distill something out of it to keep ourselves going until the UN can send another expedition?"

Dr. Rhodes shook his head. "In the first place, we simply don't have the fuel. I doubt if the boat we have could even clear Mimas before it was empty. In the second place, it would probably be years before the UN got around to sending a new expedition. In the third place . . . well, maybe Titan would give us hope, but it's so very unlikely that it's no good to dream about it. We have to face it. We're here on Mimas to stay."

He walked around the little tent a bit. "As I see it, the only thing we can do now is to write down all our findings so that the next expedition will know. I think I shall do that in the time we have left."

Bruce nodded slowly. "That is if there is an Earth left to send an expedition, if Terraluna is not stopped."

Dr. Rhodes nodded silently, sat down at the little folding table and drew his notebook from his spacesuit pocket. "I may as well start. Suppose you go out and do some more exploring. May as well make the most of it."

Bruce watched his father, then sealed the helmet of his own suit, and, taking a couple of tools along to pry aside rocks and poke the ground, he unzipped the tent and quickly stepped out.

Outside, he started walking toward the site of the

ancient ruins. As he walked he noticed a depression in the ground and realized that it marked the spot where the space ship had rested. Idly he walked over to the long shallow groove where the ship had slid to a stop and where its weight had gradually pressed the dust of the plain down.

Suddenly Bruce stopped, stared hard. It seemed to him that in the center of the shallow depression there was a slightly rounded bump that seemed to give off a metallic gleam.

Swiftly he made his way there. Sure enough, the ship had pressed away enough of the time-old dust to reveal something. Bruce knelt by it, pushed aside the gray dust with his hands and found himself brushing the top of what seemed like a metallic rounded surface.

Excitedly, he clicked on his helmet phone. "Dad!" he called sharply into it. "Come out here and see what I've found. Something very odd!"

His father answered, and in a few minutes Bruce saw the suited figure emerge from the tent and come in his direction. Bruce drew a small crowbar from his belt, one of the tools he had brought along, and tapped the side of the metal bump.

With his second blow, he got a reaction he had never expected. The bump moved! There was a grinding vibration in the ground. The round metal surface seemed to revolve slightly and then started to rise upward. Beneath Bruce's feet the dust-caked plain started to push away, and the boy barely had time to jump widely to one side.

While his father ran to join him, Bruce stood and watched a metal cylinder rise from the ground. It came up in jerks, hesitantly, clumsily as if motivated by an uncertain and faulty mechanism. Higher and higher it rose, until it assumed the form of a cylindrical ball, several feet in diameter, rising into the air on six long metal stilts that continued to push up from the ground.

Now Dr. Rhodes joined Bruce and the two stood staring up as the mysterious globe rose a couple dozen yards above the surface. It came to a jerky stop, and the globe slowly revolved, moving within the framework of its stationary stilts.

"What is it?" gasped Bruce at last.

"Looks like a watchtower," said Dr. Rhodes. "From the way it moves, I'd say it was automatic, and very, very old. Probably dates from the ancient city's day. I wonder what it was for?"

"I guess my poking around must have finally nudged its old triggering machinery," Bruce said.

"That plus the fact that the space ship was sitting on top of it and holding it down," his father added. "Look, its side is opening up!"

Bruce followed his father's pointing finger. Sure enough, a panel in the side of the metal globe was sliding open. As they watched, a short stubby snout poked through, and suddenly there was a puff of blue flame from its end, after which it receded, and the panel closed.

"Now what was that for?" murmured Dr. Rhodes. "Looked like a shot or a signal."

Bruce took his eyes off the tower, gazed around. He gasped, grabbed his father's arm. "Look over there, in the mountains on the edge of the plain!"

There was a dust cloud hanging there, a glowing mushroom-shaped cloud that had no business in the airless void of Mimas. Where there had once been a jagged mountaintop, one of the chain on their close horizon, was now just a gap.

"It was an atomic shell!" Bruce yelled. "There's an atomic cannon up there!"

Chapter 17 The Eternal Watchman

THEY stood and watched the faraway cloud vanish rapidly in the airlessness of Mimas. A few seconds afterward they felt a slight vibration in the ground as the shock finally reached them. "It was a very mild atomic explosion," said Dr. Rhodes finally. "Very mild. I would say that it was unusually weak. After all, with the low gravity here, a really high-powered A-bomb would have blown much more than that mountaintop to pieces."

"That would mean that the cannon was loaded long ago, that maybe the shot was accidentally triggered off," suggested Bruce.

"I hope so," said his father. "I can't believe there are beings still living here. I would rather say that this whole tower and gun were automatic, waiting here for countless ages for something to trip it off."

"Our space ship landing on top of it must have started it, and my banging on it afterward finished the job. Sure must have been old and stuck to have been so slow in reacting," was Bruce's comment.

Dr. Rhodes walked back to the place where the tower had emerged, was fingering one of the long metal stilts on which the ball housing the cannon was resting. "Yes, from the pitmarks in this metal, I would say it is a miracle that the whole thing has not long ago dissolved into dust. This structure must be as old as the city here, as old as the ruins in the rings!"

Bruce looked at the aged-appearing metal rods and saw what was meant. There was no polish on the structure, every bit of the surface seemed pocked and darkened and dead-looking. He expressed this thought to his father, who replied:

"That's true, Bruce. Back on Earth we know that metal can weaken from time, no matter how hard and how toughened. And in millions of years . . . well, see for yourself."

Bruce now dropped to his knees and gazed into the space from where the structure had emerged. There was a hole in the ground, below that tower, a pit leading downward into darkness.

"What do you suppose is down there?" he said.

Dr. Rhodes looked down. "Let's go and see. Get a rope from the tent."

Bruce got to his feet, raced back. On the way, he

said over his helmet phones, "It may be very dangerous. Suppose we find creatures down there, creatures that may be deadly?"

Dr. Rhodes' voice came over his phone, "What have we got to lose?"

As Bruce scooped up the rope, his father's remark recalled to him the desperateness of their position. But, down in that hole, underneath the surface, perhaps they might find something that would help them.

Back at the pit beneath the guard tower, they tied one end of the rope to a boulder sticking from the ground and then dropped the other end down the pit. Bruce switched on the lamp that swung from his spacesuit's belt, and then slipped into the hole and down into the darkness. His father followed him closely.

The hole was no deeper than the height of the tower that had arisen from it. At the bottom, they stood on a pockmarked metal slab and looked about. To one side a door-sized gap opened upon blackness.

Bruce flashed his light. It shone down a long corridor, at the end of which he seemed to see a cavern-like space. He mentally shrugged off the chill that struck him, remembered that they had nothing at all to lose, and started off down the corridor, followed by Dr. Rhodes.

The walls of the place seemed to have been cut out of rock with no markings. When they reached the entry to the area at the end, they stood and flashed their lights.

It was a wide chamber, very wide, and stretched into the darkness beyond the reach of their beams.

All about them they could see odd-shaped boxes of stone. When Bruce looked closely at the nearest one he realized that it was the same size and form as the unearthly coffin in the tomb on the ring-moonlet. These were coffins containing the bodies of the last inhabitants of the Saturnian moons.

They walked on, side by side, through this hall of the dead. At one place, part of the wall had fallen through and tumbled a number of the odd boxes. Several had been broken open and Bruce could not help but glance inside.

There was nothing there, nothing but some fine gray dust. Of the appearance of the bodies, time had erased everything.

They walked on. Gradually the array of coffins came to an end and was replaced by various boxes and containers and piles of things. This was evidently a storeroom, but nothing could be made of what had been stored there. Vague outlines that seemed to suggest things such as clothing and perhaps food, but all, all was gray dust. When they touched anything, it simply shifted apart and flowed gently onto the ground. Some parts made of plastic remained intact and fell in shards and splinters. Here and there a bit of metal failed to fall apart.

Dr. Rhodes sighed. "I had hoped we could find something of use to us, but I am greatly afraid there will be only dust."

"We must keep looking, Dad," said Bruce. "Maybe something was intended to last . . . Hello, here's the end."

They had come to what was apparently the end of the cavern hall. Before them was a flat, polished, black surface. "Looks like a coating of something on this wall," observed the old engineer. "Notice that the other walls are rough and unfinished."

He reached out a hand, touched the wall, noted its smoothness, its absence of pocks and time scars. He took his short explorer-pick and tapped the wall. Instantly there was a crack and wide rays of breaking spread along the flat surface. "Ah, ha!" said Dr. Rhodes, and hit the wall sharply.

It broke apart like thin glass. As it fell, there was a sudden swoosh of air past their helmets, a brief but hard wind as imprisoned air escaped from beyond the cracked wall into the airlessness of Mimas. When the blowing stopped, they flashed their lights beyond.

They saw a second cavern hall before them. But this was different. This was shiny and bright as if almost new. Dust there was, but it did not conceal the state of preservation of what they saw.

It was machinery, metal objects standing on platforms, objects standing on rollers, devices that must have been used to make things. They walked into the new cavern and looked with wonder.

There was no storeroom of clothing or food here; it was a deposit of scientific achievement. Some of the devices seemed to be understandable. There were several that looked as if they could be used for digging, others obviously made things, for it could be seen where there were spaces for inserting raw materials and chutes for discharging a finished product. A number of devices seemed designed to serve as cars, for they had series of interlocking wheels that probably were used to roll the vehicle.

They walked on, examining, speculating. Dr. Rhodes paused before one device, studied it a minute and then reached out and pulled a lever, one of the few instances where something like an identifiable starting mechanism appeared.

For a moment nothing happened. Then there was a grinding sound as if some hidden wheels inside the thing were moving. A chugging was apparent in the vibrations in the floor. There was a little flare of electricity, and the sound stopped and the machine lapsed into silence again.

"Hmm," said Dr. Rhodes, "that was very interesting. These things still have some power left in them—but not enough apparently to do too much. I suppose some sort of atomic battery powered them, and even after all this time, a charge remained."

"What do you suppose the thing did?" asked Bruce.

His father shook his head. "Heaven alone knows now," he said. "I'm afraid that a civilization of non-humans would have needs we might never guess. It will take Earth's engineers a long time to work it out, for they'll have to take it apart. You and I will probably never know."

Bruce said sharply, "Let's not talk like that. Maybe there's something here we can use to help us. Perhaps there's atomic fuel here or something?"

"Very unlikely, in fact almost impossible," said his father. "You see, even the most powerful radioactive

substances have a definite lifetime, and die out . . ."
He stopped short, exclaimed, "What was that?"

Bruce had heard it too—or rather felt it. A grinding
noise in the ground, a sound as if something were rolling in the darkness, rolling toward them!

They turned to the source of the sound, but a number of bulky machines blocked their light. They felt
the sound coming nearer, echoing through the stone
floor and the soles of their metal shoes.

Then, around the corner of darkness there appeared
a beam of reddish light, and behind it the metal front
of a tall cylinder. As it came closer, they saw that the
cylinder was mounted on a series of flat rollers. The
light came from a spot somewhere in the cylinder's
center. Sprouting from the top and sides were a number of snakelike metallic arms waving toward them.

"Run!" Bruce shouted. "The thing's a robot watchman! Don't let it touch us!" He grabbed his father,
and they started to run into the further darkness of
the hall, while behind them the robot cylinder chugged
and swung, its speed increasing slightly.

The two ran on into the darkness, past machines
and exhibits that seemed to be gaining in size as they
went deeper into the cavern. Behind them the red light
of the pursuing robot was gaining slowly and its blood-
colored glow cast a frightening light on the huge
machines that stood in age-old silence in this lost
cavern.

They had run for perhaps several hundred yards,
and now only tremendous pieces of machinery stood
around them. Bruce saw what looked like a huge con-

struction machine, a towering device that seemed, as he ran past, to combine the qualities of a steam shovel with those of a concrete mixer. He caught glimpses of spouts on others, and big sweepers, and a device that looked like a tremendous land-boat mounted on dozens of giant rollers.

Now the robot was very close to them, and Bruce imagined they could almost feel the waving tips of its tentacles. They came at last to a tremendous thing that stretched across the cavern and blocked any further view. They dashed up to it breathlessly and turned, their backs to it, determined to make a desperate effort to beat off the guard robot with their bars and picks.

But Bruce was surprised to see that it was not as close to them as he had imagined. In fact, it was several yards behind and moving more slowly than when they had first sighted it.

As he watched, the robot rocked slowly toward them, seemed to move hesitantly, uncertainly. Its tentacles stopped waving, began to droop, its light flickered.

Then the robot came to a complete halt only a few more feet away. A tentacle waved uncertainly in their direction, the red beam flared up a bit sharply and then unexpectedly cut off.

For a moment they stood in darkness and in silence. In the whole mysterious cavern nothing moved.

Chapter 18 The Golden Ship

BRUCE stood and waited. Over his earphones came only the sound of his father breathing. In the cavern before them there was pitch darkness. He reached a hand down and switched on his belt light.

The beam shot out. Instantly they saw the robot. It was only a few feet away from them, apparently staring at them, motionless.

For a few seconds they stared back at it silently. Bruce whispered, "Its light is out. It isn't moving. It looks sort of dead to me."

"Maybe it's a trick," was his father's whispered reply.

Bruce lifted a hand slowly. There was no response from the robot. Then he lifted his crowbar, reached

174

out with it slowly and finally touched the metal surface
of the cylinder body. There was no response.

Emboldened, he reached out further, poked at the
thing, nudged its tentacles, which were hanging lifeless. He got no response. "I think it's run down," he
said, "just like a toy with a spring engine."

His father moved, walked slowly toward it, reached
out a hand and grabbed a tentacle. The limp, metallic,
hoselike thing was lifeless in his grip. Bruce tentatively
tapped the light socket in the creature's "head." But
still nothing.

"You're right," Dr. Rhodes finally explained. "It
has actually run down! I never thought to live to see
such a thing. Do you know what this means?"

"Why, Dad? What's so remarkable about that?"
Bruce said, walking around the creature to examine
it on all sides.

"We've actually seen an atomic battery reach its
end, Bruce! Don't you remember your lessons on radioactivity and the tables on the half-life of various
substances?"

"So?" Bruce asked, still mystified.

"Atomically activated material remains charged and
active for various periods of time. Some substances
when so charged lose half their charge in a few
hours or a few days, but all the heavy elements that
go into our atomic batteries have their half-life period
over thousands and even millions of years! You've
seen the so-called perpetual lights and clocks on the
market, advertised as good forever. Well, of course,
nothing can go on forever, but those lights and clocks

—like the battery in your space suit—actually do go on discharging their current for millions of years. That's one of the real miracles of our twenty-first century Atomic Age.

"Well, here is a robot machine that must have been operating on some such battery—and it has finally run down! Do you realize all the millions of years that this watchman-machine has been standing in this underground museum motionless, waiting for an intruder? And when one finally comes, we two, it has just enough power left to start up, chase us a bit, and finally exhaust its charge entirely and die!"

Bruce nodded to himself. It was something awesome when you looked at it that way. "Why is everything in this part of the cavern so well preserved compared to outside?" he asked.

His father replied slowly, "I wish I knew. There was some sort of gas that rushed out when we broke the seal on this section. It must have had some effect in delaying the aging of metal. I wish we had been able to capture some of that gas—would have been a big discovery itself."

"Yes, if we could ever bring any of this knowledge home, Dad," Bruce replied. "Let's look around so we can write down everything we see for whoever finds us—or our bodies." He shuddered as he said the last, but he was determined to carry on.

"Yes," his father said. "For instance, what's this end thing? I think we passed some big construction machines, some sort of land-buses, and so forth, but this one at the end we haven't seen."

They turned their backs on the lifeless robot and looked at the huge device that filled the end of the cavern, which was the last thing in the great underground storehouse of the last survivors of Mimas.

They turned their lights on it and saw a huge metal and plastic rack, stretching from one wall to the other. Something gleaming and golden was mounted on that rack, way over their heads. Bruce looked up, saw a little platform up there. His weight on Mimas being so slight, he knew he could jump up to it. Obtaining his father's consent, he bent his knees and leaped.

He caught the edge of the platform easily and found himself standing beside a circular doorway set in a huge metal cylindrical thing that towered up to the top of the cavern and whose base was sunk deep in the framework of the supporting rack. A wild notion struck Bruce as he caught the outlines of the thing. He reached out, pushed on the doorlike disk. After a few prods, it swung aside. Inside the cylinder he caught a glimpse of spidery runways, of beams and tubes, and he called excitedly to his father, "It looks like a space ship!"

"What!" In the next moment Dr. Rhodes had jumped up and the two of them were pushing inside the strange construction and examining it.

There was no doubt about it. They had found a space ship of the ancient men of Saturn's lost moon, standing as the last and final exhibit in their civilization's tomb. As they made their way excitedly around the inside of the great craft, they noticed the differences and the similarities to the ships of Earth.

For one thing, this craft seemed to lack any division into rooms or sections. The crew evidently walked along weird beams and trapezes around a hollow interior. Fully exposed to view were the rocket tubes, the fuel tanks mounted to the framework, the mixing chambers. Up at the head of the ship, a set of trapezes were suspended before a series of rods and handles that were obviously the controls. Other strange racks and spaces were about them, whose purpose defied their guesses.

"What kind of creatures were these, anyway?" Bruce remarked as he jumped lightly from catwalk to beam to gaze out of what had once been a porthole but was now a hollow hole in the surface, whose transparent substance had probably vanished into dust and gas an eternity ago.

"I would hate to speculate on it," said his father, who was studying the rocket tubes in the rear. "I get the odd feeling that they combined the qualities of monkeys with those of spiders—with maybe a suggestion of something shelled as well. They built their robot with tentacles rather than hands, and it didn't move on legs or wheels, but rather on rollers. No human culture would probably build in that fashion. But, Bruce, you should look at these rocket tubes, they're absolutely amazing!"

"How's that?" said Bruce making his way back to the lower end.

"These tubes are still in perfect condition . . . because they are diamond! Look," his father pointed along the outline of the huge blasting rockets, "these are actually cast of one single diamond—a perfect substance for rocket tubes!"

"Where would they get diamonds that large?" Bruce asked, running his hand over the glassy-smooth surface of the glistening white crystalline tube.

"Easy," his father said. "With atomic furnaces, they could make them under intense sun-hot heat and extreme pressure. All they would have to do would be to make soft carbon molds and turn them to diamond in these super-furnaces. In fact, I bet we could do it on Earth too, if we set up the proper atomic fires!"

Now Bruce thought of the meaning of this ship. "Do you suppose we could make this ship run? Could we use it to go home in? You said the tubes are intact."

His father hesitated, and said slowly, "I'm afraid not. I admit the ship looks to be in good condition, the diamond rockets are perfect, and what I can make out of the rest of the ship is in good shape—although it is no longer airtight. But what would we use for fuel? We have none, and this ship has none, and any store of fuel the Mimas-men left would long ago have lost its power. If we could get fuel, I think I could make it run . . . but . . ."

Bruce followed his father as they made their way to the entry disk. Leaving the ship, Bruce tried to slide the disk shut again. He shoved it hard, and suddenly the disk slipped, cracked on its fasteners and fell off.

"That's something else," Dr. Rhodes said. "This ship's metal parts are old and 'tired.' I don't know how long it would hold up under strain."

As Bruce followed his father down, another thought struck him. "You know, Dad," he said, "this ship looked like gold. It has a gold tinge."

They started to make their way to examine the other devices in the huge cavern. "I thought so too," his father said. "In fact, it might have some gold in its alloy. Gold is a soft and rather heavy metal to make such a ship out of, but on a world as light as this, and if gold has no particular value, it might be added to an alloy to prevent rusting. It could well be."

They started to stare at the thing that resembled a land-crawler. "Gee, Dad, think of how they would stare if we could go home in a gold space ship with diamond jets!" Bruce chuckled.

"As long as we can laugh, we've got hope," his dad answered.

They started to look into the interior of the big roller-resting thing, noting again the lack of seats or flooring, only a webwork of beams and wires inside.

Suddenly there was a vibration in the cavern. Everything about them shook and rattled. There was a series of thuds and shocks that came to them through their space suits, from the ground and walls.

"An earthquake!" cried Bruce, climbing out of the contraption onto the ground of the cavern.

"We'd better get out of here and up to the surface," his father said, starting for the far entranceway.

Rapidly they made their way through the darkness of the underground storehouse, crossing the floor in long, low leaps, their belt lights flickering eerily on the odd shapes around them.

Through the torn seal on the end of the far cavern, and down past the shapeless coffins and displays for the dead, they moved rapidly and silently. They found the doorway to the outer corridor and made their way along it to where they could see the yellow glow of the Saturn-light shining down the pit beneath the sentinel-tower.

At the bottom, the rope was still there. Bruce went first, and they made their way hand over hand up the rope.

As Bruce reached the top, he poked his head over the edge of the pit, about to swing his foot up and go over to the surface. As his head emerged from the hole, he looked outward—straight into the muzzle of a machine-pistol held in the gloved hand of a crouching space-suited figure.

For a moment he stared in amazement, unable to believe his eyes.

His father brushed against his foot. "Come on," he said impatiently. "What's keeping you?"

"Take it easy, Dr. Rhodes," said a voice in their helmets. "You've got all the time in the universe. You're not going anywhere!"

Bruce recognized the voice and the face in the space helmet at the same time. It was Kurt Jennings.

Chapter 19 In Terraluna's Grip

ENNINGS reached an arm in, grabbed Bruce and heaved him out of the pit. He reached in for Dr. Rhodes next.

"Come on, Doc. You may have all the time in the universe as I said, but I don't, so up you come."

Another heave and the engineer joined his son. Another space-suited figure stood a short distance away, holding a weapon pointing their way. Bruce stared at this other man a minute, not recognizing him, until the man spoke sharply:

"Come on, Kurt, don't waste any more time on these chumps. Find out what we got to and let's get moving!"

Bruce recognized the voice of Waldron, the space-hand who had originally tried to sabotage their ship back on Earth before the take-off. His father evidently recognized him also.

"You're a nice pair of renegades. Pretending you didn't believe in the Saturn trip's possibility, trying to destroy our work, and now, here you are. A pair of sneaks and liars, and traitors to humanity to boot!" Dr. Rhodes was angry.

"Aw, shut up!" snarled Waldron. "Or I'll shut you up now with this gun!"

Jennings turned to his companion. "Take it easy, Jack. Let the old boy rave. He doesn't have much more time left for it!" The renegade pilot turned to them and said, "We'd better all go back to our ship; I want to ask you a few questions."

He pointed. Following his finger, Bruce saw that a long sleek craft, as big and even better looking than the one the UN had lent his father, was standing on its runners a few hundred feet away. They started over to it, Kurt leading the way and Waldron following behind, his pistol in readiness.

"Where'd you get the ship, Jennings?" his father asked, his voice now quiet and restrained.

"Terraluna's latest and best," said Jennings. "They sent it out fast after you escaped our moon base. They figured to pick up your remains on Hidalgo, but arrived in time to pick me up from that smelly little tent you left me in."

"You got here fast," said Bruce, thinking of something that had struck him as a possibility.

"Sure did. We had only two in the crew instead of four, larger fuel tanks and less spare space. Besides, we refueled completely at Achilles." By this time they had reached the entry port of the Terraluna ship, and climbed silently inside the airlock.

There were no further words as the pressure was built up, and they all entered the little cramped quarters in the nose of the ship. For the first time in several days, Bruce and his father were able to take off their space suits and get a breath of real air under real Earth pressure.

The corporation's ship was obviously built for distance travel. It was crowded when four people were forced to occupy the nose chamber. Especially when two of them were forced to sit side by side on a narrow bench under the constant menace of the weapons held by the other two.

Waldron looked at them sneeringly. "What'll we do with them, Kurt?" he asked. "Can't take 'em with us."

Jennings looked at his comrade. "No, but if they answer a few questions, we may be able to lend them enough supplies and air to keep safe until we can return or get them a pickup." Bruce caught the look that passed between the two. He knew this was a falsehood.

Jennings turned to them. "Where's the ship? Where'd Garcia and Benz go?"

Dr. Rhodes looked at them a moment; then, ignoring the questions, asked, "Aren't you at all interested in what we've found out about the rings of Saturn? That is much more important to all of us, to you two also."

Kurt shrugged. "Frankly, I don't care what you imagine you've found. My bosses only want you to keep your nose out of their mining business until they can get their new operation started. Jack and I are satisfied that Saturn's rings have nothing to do with the matter."

"Yeah," broke in Waldron, "all that stuff is a lot of nonsense. Where's your pals hiding? They coming back to pick you up?"

Bruce wondered what would be the best reply to that. His father remained silent.

Waldron got to his feet, his face reddening. "Answer us! If you want to live, better open your traps and talk!"

Jennings looked a little pained at Waldron's manner, but Bruce noticed that he did not rebuke him.

Dr. Rhodes spoke up slowly, "It won't do you any good to ask us. Neither my son nor I have any intention of telling you. But we are both quite willing to tell you that our discoveries on the rings confirmed my theories. Go back and tell your bosses that. Tell them—"

"Shut up!" Waldron interrupted him savagely. "We ain't going to tell them a thing! We'll tell them you're dead and collect our dough and that's all!"

"Take it easy, Jack." Jennings shook his head and tried to smile at the Rhodeses as if to share their feelings at his companion's crude ways. He spoke again directly to Bruce:

"You know I like you, Bruce, and I have the greatest respect for your father. I'm very interested in what you have discovered and I'm sure it's very fascinating, but right now, if you'll just tell us where we can find your ship, we'll be glad to take back any message you want to send to Terraluna."

Bruce looked at him coldly, shook his head. "No, you don't care a fig what we've found and you don't have any intention of telling Terraluna anything but what they want to hear. Waldron is more honest than you. All he wants—and all you really want—is your 'dough.'"

"Bruce is right," said Dr. Rhodes. "If you could find our ship, you'd try to destroy it. But you can rely definitely on Garcia informing the UN of your acts. That's why you want to know where they are, but you'll never find out from us. Never!"

Jennings stood up, scowled. "O.K., if that's the way you want it, that's it. My guess is that they've marooned you, gone back. I'll bet they're on their way to Hidalgo, or maybe there already. So we'll just follow them and nab them there."

He turned to Waldron. "Shall we just leave them, Jack, the same way they left me?"

"Aw, we ought to shoot them now," said the other. But Jennings shook his head.

All this time Bruce had been thinking to himself how it might be possible for them to overpower the two and capture their ship. But the renegades' guns had never been off them for a moment. Jennings motioned to them to get back into their space suits.

As they fitted themselves into their suits again, Jennings said, "To show you we're not rats, we're going to leave you some extra provisions, enough for a few more days, and a small single-beam radio sender. If you change your minds about telling us where that ship is, you can tell us in the next day or so while we're still in range. We'll return for you."

Bruce knew the lie when he heard it, but he made no answer. A few days more provisions, a few days more to think of some way out of their desperate fix.

As they were getting ready to enter the airlock, Waldron suddenly spoke up, "Say, what were you doing down in that hole when we found you? Anything down there of value?"

Dr. Rhodes turned. "Perhaps. Why not come back with us and see?"

Waldron stared at him. "Heck no, we ain't sticking around. If you don't want to talk, don't. Kurt and I will look for ourselves when we blast your pals out of existence." He waved a hand. "O.K., get in that lock."

The two Rhodeses entered it, and Waldron slammed the door behind them. They heard the hiss of the air being pumped out.

As the outer lock opened, Jennings' voice came to them:

"You'll find the extra provisions stacked just outside the ship. We'll give you ten minutes to move them to safety and get out of the way. After that we're taking off to Hidalgo."

Bruce and Dr. Rhodes jumped down, found the boxes, and without further delay stacked them up between them and started carrying them off toward where their little tent and lone space boat stood far off across the plain. Because of the very low gravity on Mimas, the several big boxes which might have been very heavy on Earth were extremely light.

At a safe distance, they put their load down and watched.

Across the plain, the shining body of the Terraluna ship swung slowly about on its runners until it pointed away from Saturn in the direction in which Garcia and Benz had traveled. The glow of the great planet shone upon it in a golden bath and lit up the emblem of the moon-mining corporation which was painted upon the ship's side.

There were small streamers of vapor now coming from the great tubes in the rear. The rocket moved forward, started to slide across the plain, and Bruce felt its vibration in his feet. It occurred to him that the "earthquake" he and his father had felt while below in the underground storehouse-museum was the sound of the ship landing.

Now the glistening vessel started to move faster across the flat rocky plain. It headed toward the rim of low mountains at the near horizon.

There was a great streamer of fire from its rear and for an instant the ship started to rise above the surface, heading for the black starlit sky. Then something happened.

There was a terrific flash of blinding light, a cloud of white vapor that vanished almost instantly in the airless void, and a tremendous thud. The whole front of the ship seemed to vanish, and the rear half settled against the plain, bounced about like some gigantic tin can, and rolled to a rest.

"It . . . blew . . . up!" said Dr. Rhodes slowly. "It just blew up." The engineer stared at it with open mouth.

A suspicion struck Bruce then. He turned his head, looked at the ancient sentinel-tower looming near them. "No, Dad," he said quickly. "It didn't blow up—it was *blown* up!"

He caught a glimpse of the muzzle of the atomic cannon disappearing into the metal sphere atop the tower—and a thin wisp of vapor was trailing into the void from its end as the robot gun vanished from sight.

Chapter 20 New Wine in Old Bottles

THE two turned and stared at the ancient gun tower. "So there was more than one shot left in the cannon!" exclaimed Dr. Rhodes. "Absolutely amazing!"

Bruce looked at it and laughed. "The folks who built that didn't like visitors. It evidently fires at anything big that moves around enough. But why didn't it shoot when Jennings first landed?"

"It's rusty and old," his father said. "It takes a lot of bumping to shake its tired old mechanism enough to start it. I can't understand what keeps it up at all, considering how crumbly the other machines are from that period—those that weren't preserved in the end hall."

As if in answer to his words, a new motion began in the tower. One of the six supporting legs slowly bent and buckled. The round ball which housed the cannon and its robot controls slowly turned as its supports gave way, and part of a side opened up and bent outward. Then the whole thing seemed to twist and, slowly, in the easy gravity of Mimas, fell to the ground, bounced and came to rest, a pile of bent metal, crystalline parts, old plastics, and dust.

They walked over to the pile. Bruce poked his little crowbar into it, shoved a bit. The nose of the atomic cannon came into view—and it was still solid and intact. "Made of diamond," Bruce said, "just like the golden space-ship's rocket tubes. It didn't melt or crack."

The short, stubby gun barrel seemed to consist of glassy crystal, solid, but cloudy and dull, not like the bright gleaming polished stones of Earth's jewelry. But it was diamond all right, as the engineer explained to his son. Under heat and stress, diamonds become cloudy but retain their qualities of resistance and hardness.

"We ought to go and look at the wreck," Bruce said, his curiosity about the gun tower satisfied. "Maybe we can find something we can use."

They started over to the spot on the plain where the battered half of Jennings' ship lay. As they walked, Dr. Rhodes remarked, "It may prove lucky for us that the atomic shell that hit their ship was old and weakened by time itself. A real new atomic shell would have blown this whole end of the plain to powder. As it is, the one that hit them had only enough power to shatter half of their ship."

The plain was strewn with blackened pieces of the ship; bits of wire, twisted insulation, fragments of paper and cloth, and so on. But the rear end of the ship was less damaged than might have been supposed. Badly bent, with cracks along its seams, its tubes were twisted and its wiring tangled and torn.

There was a still hot scar in the plain, where one tube had continued to blast out its jet until the ground it touched had become volcanic lava.

Bruce and his father looked in at the wreck of the rear end. Bruce pointed a finger. "There are some tanks that haven't cracked open," he announced.

"Hmmm," his father expressed thoughtful interest. "Give me a boost, I want to get in there and look at them."

Bruce helped his father up into the body of the engine room. He watched anxiously as Dr. Rhodes poked around the place. "Anything we can use, Dad?" he finally called.

"Hmmm, yes, I think so, Bruce," his father replied. "At least three of these fuel tanks are still full and not leaking. Their reserves, I imagine. And—yes, there is a tank of compression gas here as well."

A hope struck Bruce. "Is there any way we can use those tanks? Maybe we can refuel our space boat, go to some other moon and maybe find a way to keep alive. Perhaps to Titan?"

The gray-haired engineer stood in the wreck and thought a moment. "We could do that now. With this fuel we could get to any of the other moons in our space boat. But what I am trying to figure out is some way we could use this to get to Hidalgo and Garcia."

"In the little space boat?" Bruce asked. "I thought it couldn't get up enough power to break loose of Saturn's grip."

"It can't," said his father, poking at the bolts that held one of the tanks. "What I had in mind was the big ship in the underground storehouse. The Saturnian ship. I was wondering if it would still work after all these years."

Bruce climbed up into the wreck and joined his father, who said, "Help unbolt this. We can roll the tank out onto the ground."

They managed to knock loose the remaining fastenings that held the tank to the bent wall of the wreck. Then they rolled the barrel of fuel to the edge and let it drop. It bounced but did not break. "Those plastic barrels can take a lot of beating," his father said.

The two jumped down. His father walked around the barrel, deep in thought, then looked up. "I think we ought to take the chance, Bruce. From what I saw of that golden ship down there, I am sure its engines are intact. If the sentinel gun could still get off two shots, and it was relatively unprotected all these millions of years, then that ship's engines should still be able to blast. The tubes certainly will hold up, being diamond. I imagine the main braces will hold, at least long enough for what we need."

"Is there enough fuel here for a ship that size?" asked Bruce. "And then don't forget the ship's not airtight any longer. Its port windows have vanished into dust."

"That doesn't matter so much—its not being airtight I mean," his father answered. "We'll keep our space suits on. As for the fuel, there is enough here for us to make a rendezvous with Hidalgo, I'm certain of that."

"So what are we waiting for, Dad?" asked Bruce impatiently. "Let's get this fuel over and load the ship. We can't have too much time left!"

His father agreed. Getting back into the wreck, they unbolted and rolled onto the plain the remaining two tanks of fuel and the gas cylinder. They added a number of other parts, pieces of wiring, coils, and other parts that were intact in the ruin.

Bruce then went back across the plain in a fast lope to their space boat. Getting in, he jetted it off and rolled it on its big wheels under light blast to the wreck.

He and his father then heaved the big fuel tanks on top of the little rocket boat and tied them on with rope. When the little craft was fully loaded, it seemed buried under the bulky containers, but by gently and cautiously operating its jets, Bruce managed to keep it upright and rolling on its wheels toward the pit that led to the underground storehouse. There they faced the problem of getting the fuel and parts into the cavern and to the end where the ancient space ship rested.

They knocked off their task to return to their tent, refresh themselves, pack what was essential, and renew their strength.

They left the tent up and their notes about their discoveries lying in plain sight on the low table in the middle. Should they fail to return to Earth, whoever next came to Mimas would find their evidence. Uneasily Bruce wondered whether that might not be in millions of more years—if Terraluna exploded Earth's moon before they could be stopped.

Back at the pit, they rigged up ropes and let the barrels and equipment down carefully. What would have taken a crew of men and machines to do on Earth, two men could do here, so light was the weight on this tiny moon.

Reluctantly Bruce realized they would have to abandon the space boat. He took what he could from it and added it to the pile at the base of the pit— which also included the food and radio that Jennings had left them.

Now father and son climbed down, and made their way over the pile to the short hallway leading to the caverns. They rolled the barrels of fuel before them into the outer cavern. Painstakingly they transferred the rest of the equipment. Though it was nearly weightless, it nevertheless took work to move it and the job was tiring.

Bruce had an inspiration at that point. He went on ahead past the coffins and into the end hall. There he poked among the mysterious machines on exhibit until he found one that rested on a flat platform with rollers. This he was able to push back through the cavern to where their stuff was waiting. All this time Bruce was hoping uneasily that no second robot watchman would come to life and find them, but apparently one such was all that the ancient moon-creatures had left.

The machine which Bruce had found was some kind of complicated sorting device, resting on a wide, flat platform. Reluctantly Bruce and his father broke away the gears and parts from their base and so made a roller carriage on which they piled the tanks and equipment. This made the job of moving it up to the space ship a mere matter of pushing, and they managed that without further strain.

When they finally reached the base of the launching rack on which the golden ship rested, they faced the problem of making the ship workable. Dr. Rhodes went into the ship and probed around its engines.

"I think I have the hang of this now," he called to Bruce finally. "Essentially this operates in the same way our Earth space ships work. There are some connections here that are different, but I'm not going to alter them. I think we can fuel her. Can you manage to get one of those tanks up here?"

That was easier asked than done, but by means of a hastily rigged hose they transferred the first fuel tank to the ship. Dr. Rhodes maneuvered it into feeding position, opened the cocks, and attached it to the feed chamber on the golden ship. As Bruce watched he could see the points of resemblance. Although built by creatures that did not resemble human beings, and on a world whose culture could have had little in common with mankind's ways, still the laws of science and mechanics are such that the same type of work must be done in basically the same manner.

Once they had accomplished this first connection, the rest seemed to follow in order. Between Bruce and his father, with Bruce doing most of the hard work because of his youth and greater strength, they loaded the millions-year-old ship.

The fuel tanks were all in place. Dr. Rhodes had rigged up and patched the ancient rocket feed system, determined the use of all the old parts, however oddly shaped, and adapted them to his own use. An emergency set of controls had been rigged with coils of wire and spare space-suit batteries, so that the ship could be directed from a point near the nose of the craft.

The ship had no inner compartments. It was all one big shell, and Bruce and his father climbed up and down the various struts and catwalks like a pair of monkeys. The nose of the craft was solid and thick. The portholes had evidently been set at the side, where now were gaping holes. The Rhodeses had rigged up a small platform up there behind the nose, so they could observe where they were heading and could control the unshielded engines in the rear.

The lack of shields bothered the old engineer, until he realized that the ancient builders had apparently so arranged their tanks and controls that the rays from any exposed atomic energy were directed away from the interior of the ship. As Dr. Rhodes explained, it was a definite improvement on the Earth ships and one that could be used in the future.

"Is everything all set?" asked Dr. Rhodes formally for the last time.

Bruce braced himself, his feet swinging over a girder, his back against a stanchion. He glanced below him into the depths of the ship. He noted the various bundles of stores he had tied on to likely places among the catwalks and mysterious cupboards of the old ship. Far below he saw the exposed tanks, the gleaming surface of the great diamond rocket tubes and a spider web of new wiring.

He glanced at his father, who was squatting cross-legged behind the great curving golden front of the bullet-like nose, holding in his lap a series of keys and switches rigged on a board, penciled markings noting the various connections.

Bruce felt his space helmet and suit, and all was shipshape.

"O.K.?" his father asked again.

"Ready!" Bruce called. His father nodded, seemed to hesitate an instant, then flicked a switch on his board.

Chapter 21 Breakaway

THE ship vibrated as the gyroscopic wheel in the center started to turn, sped faster. This was the gear that would keep the ship stable, controllable. In this old craft, that wheel was mounted on the central beam that ran from nose to tail of the craft. Whatever had motivated the wheel in the original machinery was unidentifiable. Instead, it was running now on the power from one of their batteries.

A thought struck Bruce now, one that he had overlooked in the stress and strain of loading. He called to his father, "What about the roof of the cavern above us? Can we crash through it?"

His father replied over the steadily increasing hum

of the gyro, "There's nothing we can do about that. I have gone on the hope that the ancient moon-men realized that too and that the roof at this point is very thin and made to be broken out of. I'm turning on the jets in eight more seconds. Hold tight!"

Bruce clung to his girder, counted eight under his breath. His father threw a second switch. There was a rumble, and the ship shook. Blasts of fumes came welling out from the base of the ship. It rocked from side to side, fighting against the momentum of the central gyroscope.

For an instant Bruce thought the take-off would be a failure. The ship seemed unable to budge. Then his father rapidly threw three more switches in succession. There was a tremendous uproar and a terrific jolt. The ship seemed to plunge upward, and Bruce felt himself jammed against the bare metal frames.

There was a rending crash, felt through the frame of the ship, as the nose tore into the top of the cavern. Then the ship ripped through and burst out into the blackness of the void that began at the very surface of airless Mimas.

Below, Bruce caught a glimpse through a hole in the side. He saw the rocky plain diminish, caught a fleeting look at the little tent standing lonely on it. Saw a crater-like hole where their golden ship had torn out from beneath, and then the scene dwindled and was lost in the hemisphere of the little moon as they moved faster and faster away from Saturn, away into the blackness of interplanetary space.

His father was crouched over the board, watching

the flickering dials that gauged their flow. Finally he looked up, craned his neck to look out in front of them through the hole in the side of the ship.

"We're at full blast, Bruce," he said finally. "Are you all right?"

"Sure, Dad," said Bruce. He gazed down into the interior of the ship, saw the flare and painful brightness of the rocket jets reflecting violently from the bare metal framework of the ship's interior. A golden glow seemed to be seeping in through the gaps in the ship's sides. Bruce glanced outside, saw that it was the great sphere of Saturn shining through their hollow and airless vessel.

Onward they moved, and to Bruce the great sphere of the ringed planet seemed to decrease in size ever so slowly. Unasked, he loosed himself from his perch, let himself down to the rear of the ship. He moved carefully from catwalk to stanchion, hanging on to the strange thin bars and trapezes on which the ancient Saturnians had moved. He tested each connection as he went, checking their installations.

The gyrowheel was firm. The various wirings seemed to be holding. He noticed that one of the trapezes had broken loose, was swinging dangerously. He worked over to it, took a wrench from his spacesuit belt and cut the rest of the trapeze loose. Then he shoved the bar out of a nearby gap in the surface, so that it floated out into empty space and fell behind as the ship moved on.

Other pieces of the craft were loosening up, he noted uneasily. He mentioned it to his father.

Dr. Rhodes said, over his helmet phones, "I was afraid of that. This whole ship is made of aged metal. It may fall apart before we ever reach Hidalgo. I'm hoping it doesn't. When you see something coming loose, try to tie it down or else get rid of it. Anything that isn't essential can be thrown out."

Bruce worked back to his perch near the nose. Through the circular gap in the hull nearest him he saw that they were passing close to Dione, the fourth moon outward. That meant that they had gone roughly a hundred thousand miles since their take-off, that they were traveling at tremendous speeds and still accelerating.

Dione was a gleaming sphere, marked with dark splotches that may have meant rocky plateaus and a patch of brightness that may have been a lake of frozen air. They soon left it behind.

Bruce noticed uneasily that the gap through which he had watched seemed to have spread a little wider. He realized that the outer hull itself was slowly tearing open. He mentioned this to his father, but there was no answer, only a shrug.

From time to time now, Bruce had to go down and cut loose other bits of the interior. A catwalk buckled. A trapeze cut loose and started floating perilously about the interior. Several bits of metal, bolts and suchlike were now floating about, and Bruce caught these when he could and threw them away.

The constant vibration of the engines and the vibration of the gyrowheel were slowly shaking the ancient ship apart. One of the barrels of fuel seemed to be twisting slowly as the girder on which one end had been roped was swinging outward. Bruce slid rapidly back to it, untied it, and fastened it to the much stronger central beam. The girder continued to swing away, flapped and bent back and fell outward into space.

By now the gaps where the various windows had once been were distinctly larger, and seams and cracks were growing along the outer shell.

"Bruce," his father called, "see if you can hammer this front panel off. It's moving out too far."

Bruce pulled himself up to the nose. Bracing himself along the inside of the solid and firm nose, he hammered out a plate that was buckling near his father. A few strong blows and it fell outward and was lost in the void.

He caught a glimpse of the misty sphere of Titan as he did so, and realized that time was passing and their speed continuing favorably. If the ship could but hold together . . .

It continued like this steadily. Bruce working around the ship, tying, cutting, bending, his attention constantly in need as the ancient craft gave way to its age. It occurred to him as he gathered loose bolts that were always floating about, that perhaps some of these were gold, perhaps even diamonds. But this was all of no consequence. Right now they were merely dangerous junk that had to be disposed of.

"How are we doing?" he thought to ask once while chasing a particularly elusive piece of metal.

"Very well," his father replied. "Better than I had

hoped for. It seems that this Saturn engine must
have some tricks to it that we haven't discovered
yet because we are making better speed than I had
estimated."

Bruce finally caught the metal, tossed it out. "That's
good," he said, "but won't that interfere with your
calculations on getting to Hidalgo?"

"Ha!" retorted his father dryly. "What calculations?
When did I ever have a chance to make any?"

"Huh!" Bruce was momentarily astonished. "But
how are we traveling then? How will you get to our
asteroid?"

His father said, "We'll go by rule of thumb and
by sight direction. Since we have fuel to spare—all
our fuel being a gift, sort of, from Terraluna—we can
afford to waste as much as we want taking a more
indirect course, taking a longer trip. This business
of carefully calculating the shortest and quickest route
to a planet is all because of having to save fuel and
time. If you had endless fuel and all the time in
the world, you could go anywhere in space without
calculations."

"Well, we certainly don't have all the time in the
world," Bruce remarked. "As a matter of fact, I'm
getting hungry."

"Sorry," said his father. "I don't know what we
can do about it in this ship. No airlock we can lock
ourselves in and snatch a bite. Maybe we can rig an
air bubble around us with some tent cloth, if we
have any."

"I think there's some among the spare rope," said Bruce, and found it. After a little trouble and some tricky acrobatics, Bruce managed to get enough of a covering about his helmet and hands so that he could snap open his helmet and pop a bite into his mouth, as well as snatch a drink from his canteen.

Working back to his father, he was able to repeat the process. "Thanks," his dad said when the tricky process was over. "I was wondering if we ourselves could hold out."

By this time the ship was free of Saturn's moon system. And by this time also the ship was pretty much of a skeleton craft. Bruce could glance in any direction and see the stars shining unopposed. The ringed planet was always in sight, its moons attending it.

More and more the loose bits of the ship fell apart. As they progressed, Bruce wondered what would be left by the time they reached Hidalgo.

One fuel tank was now empty, and he cut this adrift. "Any sign of Hidalgo?" he asked.

"Not yet," said his father, his eyes roving around the stars before the ship. "Look for a thin crescent showing up among the stars in that direction," he waved a hand and pointed.

Another section of the side plates swung outward silently and fell away into space as Bruce looked. Checking the damage, Bruce finally again stared off.

His eyes were tired, and he was tired from the constant vigilance and work. He didn't think he had been able to catch a moment's rest since the take-off. The unshielded vibration of the gyro and the blasting tubes were another steady strain.

He stared anxiously at the black star-strewn sky. Now he thought he saw the tiny crescent his father had mentioned. "Imagination," he murmured to himself, and turned his eyes away, and then back. The crescent was still there. He called to his father and Dr. Rhodes confirmed it.

"It's Hidalgo," he said. "Maybe we could call Garcia on that radio Jennings gave us?"

Bruce looked for the radio, but then he saw another bolt floating along and went for it. "No time, Dad," he said, and swung down for the new bit of wreckage.

He kept busy as the next hour passed. Finally he paused and glanced down. The bulk of the little asteroid was already filling the sky, and he saw that his father was angling down to circle the little world for a landing. He made his way to the nose and sat by his father.

"Can you see the ship?" he asked, and almost immediately answered himself, by pointing and yelling, "There it is!" Sure enough, the tiny metal gleam of their UN ship could be seen resting near the canyon that Bruce and Arpad had discovered. He thought he caught a glimpse of a figure standing near it, but it may have been a trick of his imagination.

Bruce looked around as their golden ship circled for a landing. It would probably be a crashing, skidding stop, he realized.

The craft was now a mere skeleton. A long central

beam, at one end the blunted golden nose, at the center a revolving wheel, at the end a cluster of tanks and diamond tubes and flaring jets. Two men in space suits clinging to loose ropes and bits of thin spidery girders moving among the open airless interior.

"What a shock this will be to Arpad," Bruce thought, as his father brought the spooky framework space ship down closer and closer and finally set it to rest with remarkable softness and skill. The jets shut off, the gyrowheel stopped, and Bruce and his dad flopped off onto the surface of Hidalgo. A moment later the central tube of the ancient ship bent slowly down and the whole mass collapsed in a heap of gold and diamond parts.

Bruce and his father sat there by the pile of glittering junk and laughed as the figures of Garcia and Arpad Benz came lumbering up, waving their hands in excited greeting.